FROM DECEMBER TO JULY
THE AMANDA FILE

(Things I have written for and to my friend in England)

MARTIN REGAN DOVE

SPECIAL THANKS

To Vadin Lum You for creating the front cover, and Neal Wooten for making it work. Thanks to God, the Universe or whatever power was kind enough to make me curious enough, to attempt to define all that is beauty with nothing but words. To Momma, because a mother's love is proof positive there IS a God in heaven and he or she wants us to know what love is. To Josh, Jason, Vadim, Neal, Country, Alexis, Gizel, Holly, Stephanie, Zoila, Amy, Brad, Christopher, Britton, Mr. Rice, Grant, Mr. McMahon and Darrell for all the love and friendship you have given at one time or another. You have all made me a better person; and to those I missed, my apologies but don't worry, you are there. And to Amanda…what can I say Luv? Here's your book.

ISBN 978-1-61225-310-7

Published by Mirror Publishing
Milwaukee, WI 53214
www.pagesofwonder.com

Printed in the USA

To Amanda, for without you, these pages would not exist…

"I have not loved the World, nor the World me;
I have not flattered its rank breath, nor bowed
To its idolatries a patient knee,
Nor coined my cheek to smiles,--nor cried aloud
In worship of an echo: in the crowd
They could not deem me one of such—I stood
Among them, but not of them—in a shroud
Of thoughts which were not their thoughts, and still could,
Had I not filed my mind, which thus itself subdued."

Lord Byron
Childe Harold's Pilgrimage, Canto iii, Stanza 113

TABLE OF CONTENTS

Introduction to Pieces Selected by Amanda

Short Stories:
Carl's Line
Brandon's Saturday
Morton's Luck
White Squall
Sheila's Dead

Poetry:
Alabama Summer
Copperhead Curve
Postman
Shiny Nickels
Uncle Buddy
Wine Glass
Cartas De Amor
Island Girl
Hours
Asunder
Colour
My Singer
Tomorrow
One Night
Silly Butterfly
November Dance
AM 1 Train
Big Girl
The Lost Saloon
Bug
Casing
Central Park
Tortured Soul
Journey of the Damned
Mirrors

Martin,

I'm writing this missive to you from St. Peter's churchyard in Bournemouth, and I have to say it is a typical English day…in that it is raining, gray and bloody freezing. Apt weather though, if one is going to sit in a graveyard.

The church was built between 1844 and 1879, a helpful vicar informs me; therefore my Sherlockian deduction is this: it's most famous resident must have been interred here prior to the small but impressive gray stoned church was completed. I am of course speaking about Mary Shelley, of "Frankenstein" fame. Her family hail from these parts and are still quite prevalent in the naming of roads…and pubs, holding to a connection of a Victorian past.

People walk through without realizing Mary Shelley is buried here, along with the heart of her husband, poet Percy Bysshe Shelley (which I find delightfully macabre). Hell, I would bet the kids of today have never heard of her. Frankenstein to them is merely a block-headed, bolt-necked Halloween character, or a Hollywood film creation. But a book? Nope. Let alone the groundbreaking horror novel written by an upper-class lady in a time most ladies of her station were expected to swoon at the sight of a bare table leg or a man's bushy mustache!

Of course, we live in an age kids have never read a novel not forced on them by school. Certainly most do not seem to read for the simple pleasure of hunkering down with a good book. I find this quite sad.

They are missing out I think, because our unique friendship sprung from a love of classical literature and the romantic poets, Byron in particular. We are old fashioned pen-pals in a digital age, brought together by evocative words scribbled eons ago, tangible prose transcending the years. Treasured books, often musty and worn, found in second hand book shops, discussed and digested across time zones crossing from England to America and back. What can I say? Your own poetry and conversation certainly has reignited a long sleeping beast hidden within me, and every shared word with you has been a joy.

Hmm, I sit here wondering if kids today would be able to strike a similar friendship as ours in twenty years time? If they have never read anything beyond Facebook memes concerning a grumpy cat, or Twitter threads regarding Miley Cyrus *twerking*. This is a depressing thought I refuse to dwell upon. Why should I care if 'Progress' has created a generation of mindless morons who can barely string a sentence together? A generation who converse using *text-speak*. Hell, I'll be long dead before they tear down the libraries replacing them with conveyer belt McDonalds complete with cranial plug-in super hubs catering to the morbidly obese who can't bear the thought of missing a single inane online moment. I suspect there will also be robots to feed, burp, and change said population while their thoughts tap away on surgically implanted keyboards in their brains.

I digress. Sorry, easily done. Damn my imagination!

So, as I was saying, Mary Shelley is buried here in St. Peter's church, and she was an old stomping partner of our Lord Byron. I'm looking at empty whiskey bottles stuffed under the bushes near her grave, telling of late night drinking, possibly by one of Bournemouth's homeless population, or maybe club goers not wanting an evening to end and in need of a quiet spot to continue their wooing. I think Shelley and Byron would definitely have approved. Misbehavior and laudanum often fueled their gatherings apparently. One such lost weekend produced one of the first Vampire stories, and of course, Frankenstein.

But again, I digress!

What I love about this graveyard is the romance in the story of how Mary's husband's heart came to be buried with her. The story goes: In 1822, Percy sadly drowned when his sailing boat sank during a violent storm in the Bay of La Spenzia. His body was burned upon a funeral pyre as was his wish; but his heart refused to be committed to the flame. It is said years afterward, Mary would carry his heart with her on travels, wrapped in a page of her husband's poetry; which brings me to why I am sitting here becoming soaked to the skin in an English graveyard writing to you.

Martin, if there was ever a perfect metaphor for poetry, then that is it. Poetry wraps itself around our hearts, and is carried everywhere with us. Good poetry should be effortless. And your poetry is effortlessly fabulous, like the poets of yesteryear. I know Byron would be proud of you for continuing a tradition, in a world where poetry has been forgotten.

Every poem you have ever sent me is wrapped safely around my heart…and will be as long as I live.

Which admittedly might not be so long if I continue with this predilection for sitting in English graveyards in the pouring rain thinking of poetry, illiterate kids and ass wiping robots! My lunch break is now over, so I will bid you adieu for the moment.

Yours,

Amanda x
Wednesday September 18th, 2013
Bournemouth England

"The ocean rolls between us"~ Percy Bysshe Shelley

I firmly believe we live in a fascinating world, and have always. Humans have spent centuries searching the skies for answers to questions like "Why am I here? What does this all mean? Is there a grand purpose for me to achieve? Or is it all no more than a drop of time in which I reside? And, what's for supper?" Weighty important questions them all I say, and all of them as difficult to answer (Supper not so difficult thanks to the Chinese innovations concerning take-out and delivery).

The questions historically have always outnumbered the answers, which in my opinion pretty much defines the curse or blessing in which being a human truly is. If we had all the answers then what would we do? Take up cribbage? Would we shake hands with all of our perceived enemies and say "Well old chap, glad we got that all sorted out, now we can stop dropping incendiaries on one another; by the by, what's for supper?"

No, nothing is so easy and I suppose on some level we should be thankful for that. What would life be like devoid of questions? Somewhat of a drag I would imagine, but that's me. I am a writer. Therefore I understand the towering importance of conflict; and resolution mind you. Can't have one without the other can we? And without the two, even gardening would be a bore (more so than it already is). When I say gardening I suppose I am attempting some grand metaphor (or analogy. I can't quite get those two figured out) alluding to how one must break the soil for planting, imbed seeds and seedlings, and then combat weeds, boll weevils and whatever it is feels the need to attack your lovingly placed cucumbers; the most basic form of conflict if you will.

And this is where you are probably asking yourself what exactly the hell I am talking about, and this is where I suggest you go have a drink because we are going to start discussing the ultimate conflict in humanity…emotions. But first, a commercial break (I gotta go pee).

Okay, I'm back. Where were we? Oh yeah; questions, answers, infinite truths and the such. In as much as I think the search for truth is a noble cause; when you consider Flock of Seagulls sang "I Ran" and it brilliantly defined a moment in the eighties where being fueled by cocaine and combing ones hair in the wrong direction seemed acceptable; the truth is they are a horrid band otherwise. I think it was Aristotle who said the truth is like a barn door, you can throw a stone and hit a portion of it, but you can never hit the whole thing. Of course, this was before nuclear missiles became popular to toss at barns, so Aristotle was half right.

So let us talk of emotions, and they are my friends, truth.

We've all been in love, we have all been heartbroken (and if you haven't you should redefine your idea of living) we have all had friends who faded away, and conversely those who stuck around for the long run. It is the very best part of being a human being, friendship. Through our friends we find out who we truly are, because it is our friends who get to know us and decide to like us anyway, and us them.

This book is ultimately about friendship. And emotions, the real stuff of emotions; the dirty side of feelings. Where we expose ourselves to someone in the hope they will still like us while we share, and if you will, bare; our soul. I have such a friend, and her name is Amanda. She lives far away in England, at least, far away from me, here in New York City.

I have never met Amanda in person. This is where the fascinating age we live in kicks in like a chimpanzee on methamphetamines gets sent to space (thank you Russia). I have never once been in the same room, or on the same continent now I think of it, as Amanda Louise Baverstock. Yet, due to the age we live in, we have become friends. And friends we are. Most days when I wake up there is a message from her on one of my electronic devices, and most days before I retire to my bed, I send her a missive. We call it our "Pod". And we have furnished it with mahogany dreams.

I have friends who question me concerning this relationship, they ask if it is romantic…and I always reply: "Well of course it's romantic for God's sakes! We both love Victorian poetry. What is more romantic than that?" And of course said friends roll their eyes in such a way I am sure even Keats would disapprove (and who cares, Keats gets on my nerves).

Amanda and I met, as it were; online in this new age of electronic, computational sharing of acquaintances brushing together. And somehow or some way found each other. And to be quite honest: Really? What are the chances in the seven billion people residing on this planet that two of them who love George Gordon Byron would discover one another? Two continents, oceans between them, culture separating them, nationalities not the same coming together to share a friendship? So yes, quite the fascinating age we live in if you ask me.

There is something different in getting to know a person by the word only. It is a short-cut to the heart if you ask me. Sitting across from someone at a table, or next to them perched on barstools requires of course a modicum of communication; but at the end of the day you can get up and leave. Leaving nothing more than the heat trace of your presence, the echo of your voice; the memory of words you may or may not deny due to the tequila content in which they were shared. Oddly enough, being face to face is an easier path to the convenience of friendship, as opposed to friendship itself.

And there you have it. Words are Soul. In the ether of unimportant verbal conversation they quickly dissipate into the atmosphere holding no more meaning than the air itself. But when written; oh my…do they hold a power. The power of words is the power of Love and of Soul, it is why we love; it is why we understand how we feel. For without words, how would we describe emotions? We would shake our fists over a fire at a sky without end? No, words give us our soul, allowing a Soul to be.

It is said today is only tomorrows yesterday, but is that the truth we aspire to? Words will give you your today and share with infinite tomorrows all of the yesterdays, each and every one. Amanda this book is for you. I wrote all of these things so you might know friendship is words. Soul is only words; Love is words, for all it is worth…Life is words. So keeping this all in mind, I present to you now: The Amanda File.

I'm going to be quite honest with you right now, I have no bloody idea what I am about to write. However, I have been drinking. Therefore I know whatever spark flies between my thoughts and the fingers holding this quill, words will magically appear and with any luck they will express a somewhat coherent thought (hopefully).

I suppose I should start by telling you what this book is about, and I hazard to say to you, it is not really about anything. Makes you want keep turning pages doesn't it? Well, if it helps, I am just as curious as about what I am writing as you are about what you are reading…well there was a bunch of existential horse malarkey wasn't there?

A few months ago I was talking to my publisher Neal, at the time we were putting together my last book, and I said to him I think I accidentally wrote another book. And Neal, who is an author as well, said in his normal wry and dry voice "And how exactly does one do that?" Which is where the *accidentally* point comes into play. I honestly was not trying to write another book at that time. I was losing my mind editing a book, what sort of insanity would make one attempt writing two at a time? So there you have it, it was an accident.

Anyway, as I was working on the other book, Amanda and I would chat via the internet. The foundation of our friendship, the anchor, is Victorian Poetry. I am not ashamed to say George Gordon Byron is my personal hero, and has been for as long as I can recall. Yes, I was the kid who played 'Go Fish' with the deck of cards emblazoned with poets and authors. Amanda would proofread chapters and tell me whether she liked them or not, and I am positive I was a huge annoyance due to the fact when I get started writing I will plod through it until the end, and to her credit, she stayed right there as I piled it on. And during this time period, I mentioned to her my life long hobby of writing verse.

I promise you, I have never once in my lifetime referred to myself as a poet, I rarely call myself a writer, empirical evidence aside. For me to call myself a poet would be the same as my mentioning "look a here, I have a leg". I have always written prose, because I love it, I adore the challenge, and at the end of the day I feel it is nothing more than attaching words to emotions, to experiences, to life. Life is words and words are life, it is just that simple. The only guarantee in this life we have from birth is the knowledge we will die, and the words we fill between the two is what we are. I'm not talking about only writing, words are speech, they are thought, they are the reason the awareness we are, is significant; very important in my opinion this word thing.

I started doing a bit of side writing if you will. I would write a poem or two, I even managed to produce a couple of short stories (and the beginning of a novella not included here) for no other reason than to entertain my friend Amanda. And as the time passed, it grew. I wrote of memories, I wrote of New York, I wrote of heartbreak and friendship. I penned so many thoughts I lost track of the word count and one day when I looked at it I realized I had in a short time written a small volume of work, and I had written it all for Amanda's amusement. And I rediscovered how much I truly love to twist verse.

I owe Amanda a debt of gratitude, because for whatever reason, I had forgotten how much I love writing in that format. I enjoy the idea of attempting to write and describe the impact of a tear drop, the one which slides down your cheek, the one you refuse to wipe away because it feels as good as it feels tragic. You cannot capture an emotion in a net like so many elusive butterflies, it requires words, and as Mr. Shakespeare so famously and eloquently intoned "Therein lies the rub".

I possess a writer's memory, which means I remember a great deal more than is healthy for me. This memory does not so much encompass the events of the past, but the emotions attached to them. The ebullience of a first kiss, the guilt of a forbidden one; the heart pounding happiness of seeing a friend after too long apart, the black soul regret of betraying someone, the crimson pallor of being betrayed. The ice cold blue of indifference lain upon your plate, the passion of love and the sadness of a love not returned. All of these things are what we feel, and to write them, and attempt to express them…is bliss.

Well I certainly went on there for a bit didn't I? Sorry about that, now back to business: This book is a compilation of things I have writ-

15

ten for, and to, my friend Amanda. There are also several pieces I have written over the years, but Amanda has picked out the ones she enjoys the most, and they are the ones included, thank you Amanda.

To you Reader, I make this promise: in all writing there is sophistry, it goes part and parcel with the trade. But with the exception of the short stories included in this text (Carl's line excluded), I promise to you, from the bottom of my heart, everything you read here is honest and based upon the life I have lived. In my pocket right this moment is Paw Paws Pocket Watch; many nights I have sat on the fire-escape outside of my bedroom window smoking cigarettes (and other flammables) gazing at what I refer to as Plato's Moon, all of that is real.

I am a purist of sorts when it comes to the written word; I refuse to lie to you. I want you to feel life, to feel your emotions. I invite you to get angry at me, just as much as I invite you to feel love with me. I want you to read words that make you feel the cold, the heat, the smells of life, and I want you to pick up your own quill, and leave a legacy of scribblings for all of those who love you to look upon…and maybe, a few strangers who enjoy your style. Now I'm going to go have a drink, all this writing has made me thirsty, and who knows? Maybe I'll see you at the pub.

Martin Regan Dove
July 25, 2013
New York City

THOUGHTS OF ENGLAND

An odd thing I think, and say to myself come morning
When pale light from new day invades folds in the drapes,
She has been awake hours; I hope her day lacks for wanting.

Steam from this mug of coffee,
Curls into my sleepy eyes, I fire the tip of the first cigarette of the day;
Pondering whether the afternoon tea; encouraged her morning slip
away.

The roar of this City, it's predictable morning rage,
Filters through the kitchen window, relentless sounds of urban tedium,
Again I find my thoughts far away in England.

In her cup of Earl Gray I wonder if; she spoons sugar, splashes cream
I try suppose maybe somewhere in wanton gaze, through her window
today,
In a West wind whispered she hears me say her name.

Sidewalks bounce the echo of my heels as I walk into the fray
Sounds overcome, when in thought they become mingled,
Singled, on thoughts of England; and my friend Amanda's day

A child one time I tried to catch a rabbit, quick as silver it was gone,
Leaving only a silk warm memory of its flank upon my skin,
Not loss, but a phantom sensation, a memory; I now ascribe to Eng-
land.

Amanda…Creature of cerebral friendship, shared interest infinitum,
Her mind a canvas sharing, bright oils reflecting light, is what I see,
Portrait of a beautiful little girl caught in time…staring at me.

Penning our oft letters, laughing together voices unheard,
Earth revolving, orbiting a sun no less brilliant than the smile she wears,

In my mind

Frolicsome pair as we cross quills over oceans uncaring,
While her portrait my imagination created; center piece the gallery of
my mind,
Richer for her friendship, made better through her missives,

Someday might we meet I hope and because:
Wealth I knew not absent till Ms. Baverstock unintending,
Shown my head may lie on a pillow in Manhattan…but my thoughts
are of England.

OURS

A misty realm is where we often meet,
One dark, sometimes light, each of us owning; yet cannot share
And our letters link,
Our fingers together in little more than air

Thoughts sailing to familiar harbor
Comfort of the blind,
Touching a door known as home
Not seeing, just feeling, a sigh alone.

There is majesty in this communiqué
Would be difficult to describe
For who shares hearts and souls,
But Poets and Scribes?

Absence is glory, in letters and words,
Where a heart finds easier definition
While plight is of no immediate kind,
Similar thoughts are to find a common mind.

What a thing to share!
In lives lived and lost and found again!
The soul, the spirit, the lost newly found!
Within our quills we share a common ground.

Where we live the often standing absent; yet near touching each other
Ours…but for oceans sprawling between us
The quill and the ink scrawls on pages our very blood,
I sing to the heavens; for friendship is Love.

PAWPAW'S POCKET WATCH

It ain't a fancy watch, just a clock
Attached to the end of a brass chain

Clips to my belt loop and hangs into my pocket
Got to wind it every day, runs slow so I have to change the time weekly

I'm told it is an antique, a work of superb craftsmanship
I pull it out to see what time it is when I feel the need.

Made in Pennsylvania after the Great Depression
Cost a lot at the time, an indulgence if you will

A purchase at the time had to consider as,
Beyond discretionary, flirting with fancy; just a ticking clock

I hold it to my ear late in the evening to hear the tick tick ticking,
Before I turn out the light

And search for a sleep sometimes hiding far away in the night,
Tick tick ticking through memories of a man.

Who with no more than ruffling a boy's hair taught love; a memory
From the land of Childhood so far away now; so far, far away

A watch in my pocket attached to a brass chain,
Gives me the time when I need it

Pawpaw was wearing this pocket watch when he died,
What seems a thousand lifetimes ago.

Now I wear it. Look at it to see if it is time for lunch or dinner
Or to go have a drink…out of my pocket into my hand, there's the time.

It ain't a fancy watch, just a clock
Attached to a brass chain, ending with a time telling teardrop…

The sensation was that of a smothering heat. Like a furnace, like the outcome of a preacher's threat of hell. A growl in the distance, the quiet rumble of a great beast; and then another…and another. A crescendo of ferocious hungry screams building in number and volume. A primitive helpless bone chilling fear crawling in the bowels, and the terrifying, tear inducing fright of climbing over the feral howls. A chattering frozen spine of fear cutting through the darkness, accompanied by the desire to scream until the world stops…

Kyle's eyes flashed open even as he felt the scream forming upon his lips. Again he was covered in sweat, sheets stuck damply to his chest and in a tangle around his legs; he had experienced the dream again. He swung his legs over the edge of the bed so he might sit up. He was trembling so violently he could not adjust the flame from his Zippo to light the cigarette he placed in between his lips. He snapped the lighter closed in frustration, hearing it's distinctive *klink* echo through the room. He could feel the dampness of his cheeks from fear-tears.

This was the dream. That damnable dream he could never re-member, the one which was systematically ruining his life. He stumbled to the bathroom and ran water into the sink, splashed it onto his face until he could think clearly. He gazed into the mirror, haunted brown eyes gazing back at him. He tried to avoid noticing the gray hair streak-ing from his temples, the bluish bags under his eyes, and the ashen caste covering his once robust complexion.

If he could only remember the dream and why it was so fright-ening, what did it mean? These were the questions he so often asked himself while standing at the morning sink. He looked back into the bedroom at the empty bed with its twisted sheets, blanket tossed to the floor. A digital clock on the nightstand read three forty five AM. He sighed knowing he would not get back to sleep now and shambled into the kitchen to make coffee.

There was a time, shifts of housemen were there at all hours to cater to his needs; but when the children went to University and Brenda left to find her own peace from his indefinable night terrors

21

which grown at a terrible rate and frequency…he found them all employment in other suitable households so he may be left alone with his nightmares.

Kyle was wealthy. Not rich, but wealthy. He was so wealthy he had never once in his life noticed the wealth. In the way other people felt about oxygen. Rarely noticed, completely taken for granted as it is so *there*. He would have never in a lifetime mention being *rich*; that was the sort of thing crass American's said on commercial cruises while drinking champagne after winning the Lottery. No, Kyle was from real wealth. A wealth began questionably in a past far away when his family was angered over Dicken's poor portrayal of factories in their ownership.

But that was far away from Kyle. His existence was a luxury now afforded by global investments and banks with his name emblazoned upon them. There was never a thought or recollection of dismal factories filled with the hungry poor working for next to nothing, or mines being dug out by the living dead for what is now referred to as the pursuit of blood diamonds. Now everything was white glove portfolios and silk suits fitting to perfection; the idle class if you will.

Not to say Kyle didn't work. He almost daily went to an office located in a glass high rise in Manhattan. He attended Board meetings (or *Bored* meetings as he referred to them), dined with others of his ilk, and led what he considered to be an inauspicious lifestyle. Life, if not good, was extremely tolerable…until the dreams began. And his world, bit by bit, began to unravel.

He was stirring his second cup of coffee when the phone rang. He looked at the screen on the device, it was Brenda. Realizing she was in England, he did a mental calculation, it was nearing noon there, and he was guessing she was a brunch with a G&T. He answered the phone: "Hallo?" Brenda's voice was clear over the line "Good Morning luv! I was hoping you would be asleep, the dream again?"

"Yes bloody hell, the dream" he replied. He could hear soft tinny music in the background as she said "I'm so sorry Kyle, have you given any thought to my suggestion?"

He sighed, "A head doctor Brenda? I'm not sure if I'm up for one" She laughed: "Stubborn prig. You know I haven't left you; I just need you to work this out. And again; I have the perfect referral"

Kyle looked over his coffee cup at the faint reflection of his haggard self in the window pane and said: "So luv, where are you? London?" There was a moment of silence over the line.

"Changing the subject on me I see, but if you must know, I am in Bournemouth" Kyle gave a start: "Bournemouth. Are you lost?"

Brenda giggled, "No I am not lost. I'm visiting Mandy. You remember her don't you? We met in Saudi a million years ago"

Kyle thought for a moment: "You mean the one with bright hair, red or orange or something?"

"Yes darling. And she is not a *one*. She is a dear, dear friend and is very expressive when it comes to her hair. We've been busy molding corsets of all things. I actually look quite busty wearing one of them".

'Oh right' he remembered: "Well, tell her I said hello. Is she still with that bank?" Brenda said "Yes, and terribly uninterested in working for you in America. She says the place is absolutely devoid of poets and romance, she prefers England".

Kyle thought a bit and said: "You never know, there could be a Byron in hiding here" He could hear the ladies laughing as Brenda recounted what he said. "Well Kyle, Mandy says if there is, she expects her name to be in poetry and to tell the budding Byron, if he is American, to attempt spelling Baverstock correctly"

Now it was Kyle's turn to laugh. He said "Tell her I think she has undue expectations from our American friends" and they laughed together for a moment.

There was another brief silence over the line, and Brenda said "Look Kyle, I know how bloody stubborn you are, but I honestly think you should give this Doctor a try. What could it hurt? This dream, whatever it is, is not healthy. Your wife and children will eventually need you again. To be quite blunt old chap, I am BEGGING you"

Kyle ran his fingers through his hair, but before he could reply she said "Look, I placed the woman's business card in your wallet months ago behind the Master Card you never use. She is very discreet and on the Upper West Side. Would you give her a ring please?"

He exhaled dramatically, "Alright Brenda, I'll think about it" He heard her make a noise sounding like a squee!

She said "Please, please, please! And now Mandy's broken out a bottle of Talisker, which may prove to be a terribly wonderful idea. So I am running" and in a quieter voice she whispered "I love you dearly. Find out what this dream is and fix it so we can have our lives back" and then louder "Alright luv! Boarding the whiskey trolley, chat with you soon!" The line went dead.

Kyle sat in the back seats of the limousine. A plush black leather cocoon surround by darkened windows dimly reflecting a passing city. He told the driver there was no stop today, just drive through Manhattan from top to bottom, he didn't care the streets and desired no destination. He craved the movement. He was sure the driver thought him insane; and perhaps he was. He sat pondering the dream. Everyone has dreams he supposed, he remembered a cousin who would often regale everyone near with a recounting of his own, literally driving anyone within hearing up the fence. Who cares? Thought Kyle, it is only a dream. Everyone has them.

'Damn it! Why is it I can't recall this one?' It frustrated Kyle to no end. He had become a zombie of sorts, stumbling around in an exhaustion caused not from activity, but from lack of sleep. It was going on five years now he reckoned. It started slow, a nightmare. It shook him from his sleep, and yes, a bit frightening. But with no recall came no concern. It was frequency he considered, brought him to this place, sitting in the backseat of a car traveling to nowhere and avoiding all of the somewhere which was available.

The dream had grown. And not being able to remember any real details of it was the thing he thought: made it eventually more terrifying than he assumed it actually was. Frustration! Makes you want to smash furniture and break glass he thought. Not due to the desire for vandalism, but sheer and perfect anger from lack of understanding. The time had passed and the dream came to visit more often. Frequency, again he thought. It slowly had climbed from bemusement to aggravation, to anger, and eventually…Fear.

'It will suck the sap out of your bones' he thought, to be frightened of sleep. And there it was, after years of this dream: he would rather do anything other than go to bed. A nap in the office would be supplemented by a nap in the back of the car. To nod off at dinner with the family in mid conversation because the idea of trying to sleep in the bedroom is anathema; try explaining *that* to the wife.

The car was passing 125th Street and Broadway as Kyle reached towards the mini-bar thinking he might pour a scotch. When he reached to open the tiny fridge for ice he felt the bulge of his wallet slide against his chest within the inside of his jacket pocket. He leaned back into the seat forgetting the scotch. He retrieved his wallet. After opening it discovered just as Brenda had said; a business card nestled behind the credit card he never used. Dr. Israela Cohen, office in the west seventies. He stared out the window of the car while it paused at an intersection and watched a flock of pigeons in an aerial ballet choreographed by nature fly in looping swirls around and over power-lines to land on window ledges of the adjacent buildings. He thought to himself: 'To be so free'.

Hot…Heat like an oven. Consuming you entirely, an ice-cube my God! Would be tantamount to heaven in this inferno; so very hot, the kind of heat where even your sweat is dry, and the growling…what is that?! Oh, oh, oh my God in heaven! Climbing! Climbing and climbing heat forgotten, fear-tears popping out of your face! Panic!! Howling screams denoting a furious hunger; and Fear. Hopeless Fear turning your soul inside-out. Panic!! Climbing up and up, over howling roars, howling! So many, so very, very many! A churning terror screaming and echoing in your mind, bouncing around the inside of your head! So many!!

Kyle woke up with bile on his tongue. He coughed, throat dry, and knew instinctively he had been screaming. Again the sheets were twisted and sticking to the sweat exuding from every pore of his body. Again he peeled himself out of his own bed, out of the unremembered but terrifying nightmare visiting again.

"This is Dr. Cohen" Kyle looked at the phone in his hand slightly confused. He expected a secretary, at the very least a receptionist to answer the phone. He said "Uh, I would like to make an appointment with Dr. Cohen?"

"This is she"

Kyle stuttered "My wife recommended you. I am, uh, having an issue with dreams" there was a pause on the line and she said "Dreams of a specific nature? Or dreams in general?" he sighed, "I don't know. I can never remember this one, and it is, well, it is sort of wrecking my life"

"Are you free Wednesday? Around two-ish?"

Kyle replied: "Yes"

Kyle walked up to the ornate building on Riverside Drive in the seventies. There was a cold wind blowing off of the river ruffling his coat and hair. The doorman directed him to the elevator that would take him to the appropriate floor. He was expecting an antiseptic Doctors office but was surprised when the door was opened by a woman in her sixties wearing a navy blue dress, string of pearls around her neck, and she was barefoot. "Dr. Cohen?" he said.

She smiled "Yes, please come in"

There was a Baby Grand piano shining in a certain polished splendor sitting by the French windows. The room was not large by any stretch of the imagination, but was tastefully furnished, there was art on the walls Kyle was reasonably sure was authentic. She invited him to sit on the sofa, and sat in a chair almost facing him.

"Kyle, your wife was a student of mine years ago, and she mentioned some time ago at a party she would like for you to speak with me. I told her on no uncertain terms this would be by your choice. I am retired and have garnished a great deal of success in my field, but to be honest with you, I am not so secure in my retirement I would turn down a client; especially one who Brenda feels so strongly about"

Kyle was nonplussed. He sat for a moment in quiet inventory of the reasons he walked through this door in the first place, and made a decision.

"Dr. Cohen, I think maybe, maybe…well hell. I need some bloody help"

She looked at him reflectively and said "Do you mind if I smoke?"

"Bloody hell, no! I'll join you if you wouldn't mind"

She stood up and walked to a cabinet. Upon returning she placed a crystal ashtray on the table and offered him a Dunhill. Cigarettes both lit and smoking she said

"Tell me about this dream"

Kyle leaned back on the sofa exhaling a plume of smoke "The whole thing has me knackered to tell you the truth. It started several years ago. At first it was just the night shivers I thought, and I could never remember what was frightening me when I woke up"

Dr. Cohen looked at him directly, "You have no memory what-so-ever of the dream itself?"

"Nothing, not anything; I wake up screaming, I wake up wrapped in sheets. Bloody well drove Brenda off the ledge, and I don't blame her. In the beginning she was understanding, nightmares and all, but as time went by it started driving her away. What is so frightening in my life to cause this? It's a mystery. I'm being open because I can't stand it anymore. I'm afraid to go to sleep in my bed. I just wish I knew what it was. I have absolutely no recollection at all. The not knowing is as much a frustration as the nightmare itself"

Dr. Cohen lit another cigarette "So you are saying" she murmured "For the last several years you have been suffering from a nightmare you cannot remember, but has become the forefront of your life?"

Kyle sighed "I am afraid to go to sleep, because I know I will wake up in terror and have no idea why"

"Can you tell me anything at all about the dream, sensations, impressions, anything?"

Kyle palmed his forehead, running his hand through his hair "That's the damn thing. There is nothing but fright, the sweat, the screaming; but nothing else. I wake up terrified of…nothing as far as I can tell. I am losing my wife, my kids; my sanity, all because of this dream I can't remember"

Dr. Cohen ground her cigarette out in the ashtray, thoughtful in the moment. "Kyle, I am going to make a suggestion. You are not required to make a decision about it today, or ever. Part of my practice is hypnotism. And I know to an Englishman this sounds like witchcraft or some other American hippie-ism for lack of a better word. I have experienced success with this in several circumstances similar to yours...I have to make something crystal clear here: if there is *any* part of your life you absolutely do not wish to revisit, this may not be an avenue you desire to go down"

Kyle sat rather stunned. He looked at the cigarette burning between his fingers; he gazed out the window and then said "Really?"

She nodded and replied "Not today Kyle. I need you to go home and think about this. If you choose to never come back I will understand completely, but, if you do decide to return...you may find what it is your mind is protecting you from. And may not thank me for it"

"But"

"No buts Kyle: go home, think it over, and if you want to pursue this course of action; you have my number" she smiled "It is not going to change anytime soon"

Kyle stood up, adjusted his jacket, flicked imaginary lint from his trousers and asked "Should I leave a check?"

She smiled and said "No, Brenda gave me a retainer"

As he was walking to the door she said "You have many who love you" He nodded his thanks and walked out the door.

'Can't be easy can it?' he thought while riding in the back of the limo. 'I go to find help, and it is some sort of mystical shyte I wasn't prepared for. Why don't I just go rub the bones of some forgotten saint in some forgotten church in nowhere? Go rub my arse against Stonehenge for Christ's sakes! Brenda and her friends are going to be the death of me' Kyle watched the sky through the sunroof seeing only white clouds against a blue nothing.

Climbing...climbing and screaming into the abyss. SCREAMING! NO, NO, NO! the growling; all of them in their hunger, feral teeth and glowing eyes; Hungry, the hunger of their howls turning your bones to water...climbing, climbing...

Kyle woke up shaking and trembling, covered in his own urine. Again filled with fear, again not remembering why; and suddenly: The thought there could be relief. He stood naked in the bathroom looking into the mirror's reflection of the wreckage left of what he used to be, wracked with a lack of sleep coupled with a fear of sleeping itself. It was time for truth. Whatever the truth might be; whatever method in which it might be delivered; these sleepless nights must end, the nightmare revealed however the method. He walked into the kitchen examining his new found honesty, the honesty of desiring a cure. He suspected this was how an alcoholic felt when he walked through the door to his first AA meeting. He did not make coffee. He instead filled the teapot, and reaching deeply into his heritage he brewed a cup of Earl Grey…waiting for the clock to tell him Dr. Cohen would be awake.

"Are you positive" she said over the phone. "Yes I am" he replied. "Then come over when it is convenient"

His driver was timely. Kyle stepped into the back seats of the car with confidence, feeling he was now ready for the truth, whatever the truth might be. Two cups of tea ingested, all the breakfast a proper Englishman requires he thought to himself. The limo passed through the morning streets like a shark through a school of fish, not hungry, but definitely noticed. Kyle watched the pedestrians walking their chosen paths through the windows, all of their destinations unknown to him, he reclined into his seat realizing his path was chosen, and he was hurtling towards the truth.

The car arrived to the address on Riverside Drive. Kyle strode purposefully though the doors, the doorman recognizing him and waving him to pass. The wait for the elevator was short. He stepped in, and rode to the correct floor. Walking to the Doctor's apartment, he felt he was ready for anything, and he felt it to his very bones. He rapped upon the door. The door opened revealing Dr. Cohen, she was wearing a brown silk dress with a paisley wrap, and she was barefoot. She invited him in.

Dr. Cohen lit a Dunhill and looked at Kyle quite seriously. "Have you thought this out properly?' she said while exhaling smoke.

He shuffled in his chair "I want it to end"

She said "Well, this may not be an end per say; but a different understanding, the gain of hidden knowledge. If anything, it will be more of a beginning than an end"

Kyle sat up rigidly straight "I don't care. Whatever this is, beginning or end I do not care, whatever it is: it must stop"

She sighed "Alright my friend, then let us figure it out"

Dr. Cohen pulled the paisley wrap from her shoulders draping it over the back of her chair. She walked to a large carved desk, rummaged around, and came back carrying a small clock and a pyramid of a wire contraption with a pendulum hanging in the center. Kyle would forever after always remember she was barefoot. Placing the clock and pendulum on the coffee table, she sat back into her chair. "Kyle, before we get started, I want to explain to you how this works, so pay attention. I am going to take you back through your life in its entirety in a very short period of time. You will not be aware of this as it is happening. When I wake you, you will not know you were asleep. I will then give you key words triggering certain memories. These memories will be real, and a part of you. Are you absolutely certain you want to do this?"

There was a heated intensity in his eyes, "Will this reveal my nightmare?"

She looked at the burning cigarette in her hand for a moment, tracking the smoke with her eyes, "More than likely" she replied.

He shifted on the couch "Alright" he muttered "Let's get to it then"

The Doctor leaned over and with a flick of her finger set the pendulum swinging. She said: "Give this a look for awhile. Don't really focus on it, enjoy your cigarette. I am going to ask a question or two. Nothing really serious; what's your middle name, who's your Mother? What's the first thing you remember? Little silly stuff you don't even know you recall. How is your cigarette? Tastes nice doesn't it?

"Kyle. Hey Kyle, how are you feeling?" Kyle looked at the Doctor quizzically. "I'm fine; why do you ask?"

She smiled. He felt it. It was the saddest smile he had ever seen on anyone's face in his life. For the first time, he felt a fear surpassing his unremembered dream. For one micro-second, he knew in his heart he wanted no answers; he would be happy with the nightmare unknown. What horrible door had he allowed to open?

She asked "Are you still interested in knowing your nightmare?" Kyle for a moment wondered if he did, but said "Yes" anyway.

The Doctor replied "Do you remember how I told you key words would take you back into time?" A bit befuddled he nodded in the affirmative. She looked him directly in the eyes and said "Are you absolutely positive?"

"YES!" he stammered, "For hells sakes yes!" and she said:

Robby

And it all came crashing down. The day; the memory, the hell his mind had chosen to forget and refused to recall. They had been in Africa, their father looking over the diamond mines: 'Legacy', as Grandfather used to say.

Kyle was nine years old and Robby seven. Two tow haired English lads traveling around with their father. One day while PaPa was away in the mines, Kyle and Robby snuck out of the camp to wander around, it was boring there. No harm, we were just running about. We were out of site of the camp, each of us portraying young Lord Greystoke. It was fun and we were laughing until…we heard the growls. The swaying of the grass was not the wind but a pride of lions. There was a tree. We heard the growling and in the ancient part of our hearts knew what it meant. We watched them as they began stalking towards us. The growling became louder, and louder until it was the screaming of lions. We ran to the tree, to the tree, and we climbed hearing those awful screams. There was nowhere to go. So many lions, howling and hungry and coming as we climbed the tree. We made it to this large branch, so many lions, so many and growling and hungry howling. One was clawing itself up the tree. It was huge and we could hear its breath. And the terror: the terror, the terror turning your soul black. And, and, and…in a moment of divine evil I pushed Robby off the branch to fall into the middle of the lions. I cannot forget his eyes. Looking up into mine as the animals began ripping him apart…in his eyes was a bewildered and terrified love. I hate myself.

And now I know my nightmare…

31

WINTER

It is a cold wind whipping between the buildings in my City,
The kind of cold reaches under your scarf to throttle you
Icy claws reminding you Nature will have her due.
She touches the pauper and prideful with the same affection
Her love the winter chill, her touch a cold wrath for you

Scurrying like so many rats looking for a warm vent,
Any respite. A train, a doorway, the office, the market
Some place she cannot follow.
Where we may gaze out of a window whispering upon it a fog
Of our breaths spelling, for this moment I escape you again.

Hands thrust deep in my pockets, head down, ears cold
I find myself walking down the hill from 134th street.
Watching for treacherous ice on the sidewalk,
I am not as young as I used to be and a fall,
Would likely hurt more than it would have twenty years ago;

Freezing cold and icy wind blowing candy wrappers,
Tiny plastic soldiers intent on mindless destinations.
There are no leaves on the trees lining the street,
Not the smallest brown wisp of memory clinging,
To the branches not long ago fervently lush and green.

The newsman on the radio cheerfully says to bundle up,
It is freezing he says, and don't forget the chill factor
His voice filled with a smile when he delivers the words,
As if we were idiots huddled by our furnaces,
Waiting to put on bathing suits and go to our workplace.

Funny how, as you become older,
Certain sensations invite memories unbidden to visit;
An ambulance screams by, siren loud and intrusive

I momentarily harbor ill thoughts for the rider inside,
If you were dead would they turn off the horrible noise?

Then I mentally kick myself as the siren fades,
Sending a prayer to whatever God may be listening
To keep watch over the Soul I just cursed,
To maybe help manufacture less intrusive sirens,
And forgive me my selfish machinations.

Sensations I think we were discussing before the noise:
Memories,
The cold touches my wrists, my neck below the chin
Inviting me a memory
The voice of an old friend;

Echoing in the recesses of my mind I hear,
The lilt of his voice, the accent;
He was British, and to my Alabama tuned ear
Sounded rather fantastic; perhaps not a Cary Grant
But the sort of voice makes one think of greater things.

An English accent will do this, in them seems to lie,
A memory of kingdoms past, of deeds bespeaking greatness;
Of Poetry and of War,
Carrying still a hint of Shakespeare in intonation,
Kipling in utterances of simple rumination;

Ah, this cold and vicious winter wind reaching around my scarf,
Creeping fingers nailed with ice grasping my tie to strangle me with:
Winter's touch;
The sidewalk gray and hard and frozen,
Reminding me of decades ago:

A similar frozen night in Denver Colorado,
Meeting at my Friend's apartment to weave an evening,

The yarn was made of cigarettes, marijuana and iced shots of vodka.
It was there the tapestry to begin,
And then off into the night to see how it would end.

The dead of winter; winds and cold, all the entertainments of the sea-
son,
Through the drapes I could see the Spanish Embassy blanketed with
snow.
I remarked it was quite beautiful,
John agreed that yes, beautiful it was,
But don't be fooled by the Spaniards, they are a bloody untrustworthy
lot.

And it was cold in his apartment, iced shots of vodka aside.
He sat, nimble fingers mixing tobacco with the weed,
Rolling a perfectly imperfect little joint;
He lit it and we passed it back and forth,
Our exhalations reflecting the cold as much as the smoke;

It was quiet as we sat at the ornate table
Nothing but the cold wind rapping upon the windows,
Warmed by the vodka, a comfortable buzz growing
He looked at nothing and said to me softly:
"Ah Martin, where are the girls of summer?"

I am getting closer to the train station now.
Still fighting the frigid wind sweeping Broadway at 134th Street
There is an old man huddled in his wheelchair,
On his ungloved fingers gold rings, one for each,
A ball cap pulled over his face only showing a mustache.

There is an echo ringing in my head,
"Martin, where are the girls of summer?"
So many years ago; lives change and we move on,
But still; a sensation will bring forth recollection

34

Oh Winter I do remember.

My God I was so young. And John was as young as I am now.
The summer he was referencing,
I was seeing a lovely stewardess named Audra
He was dating a blonde television news girl,
And then in the winter, we found ourselves alone again.

"Martin, where are the girls of summer?"
Is what I hear in my head, when the cold becomes bitter,
When the sidewalks turn gray with frost in winter,
But in truth, I am never surprised in the remembering,
No; I just look at the sky and mutter…"John, where are the girls of
summer?"

"Well, this is silly" Elaine said to no one as she sat at the kitchen table. There was a cigarette burning in a red and gold ceramic ashtray shaped like a flower, and a box of Kleenex next to her hand. She had been crying. A faint scratching broke the silence of the room, a branch from the old pine tree outside the kitchen window gently slapping against the screen, a reminder of the new fall.

Elaine stood up, mashed out her cigarette and walked over to the sink to gaze out of the window. It was a sunny day, but she knew winter was a sneaky season. It would not be long before there was a frost glazing the window glass, and all of the green in her vision would be brown. Everything has a season she thought, and then wondered if it were Shakespeare who said it, and laughed wondering how she would know anything about no Shakespeare.

She was a simple girl Elaine. Even though the faint reflection in the glass betrayed her years with gray hair, thick eyeglasses, and wrinkles; but she still thought of herself as a girl, maybe an arthritic one now, but a girl none the less. "My God" she reflected into her reflection: "No one ever thinks they will get old" and then one day you can't catch your breath like you used to, your damn feet hurt, and the doctor tells you take it easy with the coffee and onions cause your system is *changing*. She snorted to herself "Changing is a fancy word for saying you're getting old girl, no more roller coasters for you"

She began sobbing again; she couldn't help it. "Stupid dog" she whispered "You just had to go and get old and die on me". She looked over at the water bowl on the floor. It seemed lonely all of the sudden, and then realized it was she who was lonely, and cried softly into another tissue.

She named the dog Brownie, and it made sense to her husband Bob, as the mutt's coat was a mottled brown. She never told a soul she named the animal after an English poet named Browning. She was sure someone would have made fun of her, and who needed that? They lived in the country and nobody knew anything about poetry, and if they did, they didn't mention it. About the only book anybody ever talked about here was the Bible; and Elaine was pretty sure most folks didn't read that either.

She herself didn't read poetry. But one day in the library when she was a teenager she happened to pick up a book by this Browning fellow, and was surprised to see he was from England and had lived in the 1800s. This intrigued her. She wondered how folks talked back then over in another country, so she read one of his poems. She didn't remember the name of it, but it was about a Duchess who was having a painting made of her, and this Browning fellow described the process in a way made Elaine flush a little. Many years later when she got the puppy, she thought he was as cute as a picture, and it made her remember that poem. So she named him Brownie, and because he was brown, she didn't have to explain anything. All these years later she wondered why she never talked to anyone about that poem. She remembered it as being awful pretty. Maybe she should have shared it with someone. "No" she thought to herself; folks around here just wouldn't understand. But she had her dog Brownie, who was named after a famous English poet. And that was enough for her.

She sat down in the chair at the table, her back hurting from digging Brownie's grave. She planted an azalea bush over him, figuring as much as he enjoyed peeing on those bushes, it ought to make him happy having one right over him in case he needed to turn over and take a whiz. She laughed through the tears at her own silliness.

"Alright lady, when you start thinking about dead dogs having to pee; you're getting a little too close to the edge" Time to back it up a little she thought to herself. The clock read the time as late afternoon. Maybe I'll just take a hot bath now and soak these old bones. Sip a little ginger-whiskey; maybe forget about Brownie being gone for a minute. Maybe forget it all. She looked around the kitchen. The ashtray was dirty and the lunch dishes needed to be put away; "ah to hell with it, it'll keep till I get out of the bath". She could still hear the gentle scrape of a pine branch against the kitchen window screen as she trudged up the stairs.

The next morning did not come any earlier or later than it ever did. All of a sudden there it was. She opened her eyes taking in the soft early sunlight as it flirted with her bedroom windows. It was so quiet. Funny how she never noticed how quiet it was with Brownie around; his tail was always thumping against something. Or she could hear the tap/clicking of his nails on the wood floors as he rushed about the house, she might have to shush him when he barked at a squirrel in the window, he was always into something. Never was this quiet she thought. Then with a rush she remembered burying him yesterday. She sighed and climbed out of her empty bed to go to the bathroom.

The coffee maker was popping and crackling, letting her know it was nearly done brewing. She always waited for her first cup of coffee before lighting a cigarette. This made her feel virtuous in some way. She stirred in sugar and creamer powder, listening to the tinkle of the spoon inside the cup, hearing its tinny echo in the silent house. She looked out the window at the bush adorning Brownie's grave, and sat down at the table and lit a cigarette. The box of tissues was still on the table but she wouldn't need them, she had done her crying. Now it was time to get on with a new day. She exhaled smoke into the morning air, a drip tinking in the sink her only companion.

It was third Sunday. Lots to do today; may as well get started she was thinking while searching for a certain pair of shoes in the closet. There was a corn on one of her feet that had been giving her trouble lately and she wanted a pair of her old soft tennis shoes to wear. Maybe they would help, and if not help, at least not hurt too much. She put on a windbreaker, gathered her purse, ensuring her wallet and truck keys were there; and walked out the door locking it behind her. While she sat in the seat of the truck she looked over at Brownie's grave as the old engine warmed up. After awhile she put the truck in gear and backed out of the driveway.

It was a twenty minute drive into town, a quick stop for flowers and make a pickup at the pharmacy. Twenty more minutes to the cemetery. She wasn't in a hurry, no need to be. Every third Sunday she drove out to her husband Bob's grave site. She would make sure there had been no trash blown on it. She would sweep leaves off of the flat stone on the ground, and after tidying it up, leave fresh flowers. She felt it was the least she could do. He had been good her over the years, and if pressed hard, she would admit she missed him.

She walked slowly, a slight limp hindering her, towards Bob's place of rest. A breeze so gentle as to be a breath, swept the gray hair from her eyes, and a wind warm, as if a farewell from summer caressed her brow; a final kiss of apology preparing her for the coming cold, the coming winter.

She was pleased to see his stone was clear of debris. Not even a covering of browning leaves for her to brush off. She stood for a moment reading the words inscribed on the stone wondering again: "Is this all" A handful of words chiseled into a polished rock. It is pretty yes, but says nothing of who it represents. It means nothing. It is missing everything. This stupid rock telling someone when you were born and when you died: misses the whole point of the life doesn't it?

Elaine sat down next to the stone. She absently caressed his name, closing her eyes pretending she was reading Braille; attempting to fathom the tactile rub upon her fingertips. His face flashed in her minds-eye. The young Bob, the old Bob, the middle aged Bob...the sick Bob. She remembered when his hair was so thick she could barely get a comb through it when he came home dirty from the mill. She kept dwelling on the young Bob. The crooked grin he wore so naturally it would melt her heart, when his eyes were clear and his teeth were white. Back when he kissed a young girl and stole her heart from her very chest. But she remembered them all, and she loved them all. She realized she had never got her heart back, for when he stole it: he insisted upon keeping it. She was a lucky girl.

She tried to imagine what she looked like now; an old lady sitting in a graveyard alone, next to a stone with her husbands name carved on it; clutching a bouquet of flowers in wrinkled hands. She looked up into the blue sky searching for maybe a cloud to tell her something, and only hearing the conversation being held between the wind and grass, fluttering dry leaves, and she sighed.

She began to speak.

"Bob. I've never talked to you here before. Cause I know you're not here. But today, I got to say some stuff. You know I don't believe in heaven or hell, so I ain't worried about your immortal soul. I just know you're gone…and I miss you. Brownie died the day before yesterday. Don't worry, it weren't painful, he just didn't wake up. I knew he was getting old, he was gray at the muzzle and his eyes was filmed over; but he was good company right up to the end, just like you. I buried him in the backyard. I planted an azalea bush for a headstone, seemed right."

Elaine shifted. She wondered briefly what she was doing, but then continued:

"We spent a lot of years together baby, and they were good. You are some kind of man I tell you. Not many like you. When the doctor said I couldn't have no babies, I was for sure you would leave me, but you didn't. I'll never forget you telling me how it was me you married, not one single other person here or might be here. When you went to work the next day I sat in the living room and cried. I cried because I thought I was failing you. And I cried because you were so unimaginably good; I did not think you could possibly belong to me. We spent a good life didn't we? I know we did. Better than most; and here I am a silly old woman talking to the wind, dreading the drive home"

She painfully pushed herself up off of the ground and gently laid the bouquet of flowers on Bob's headstone. She kissed the tips of her fingers and pressed them against his name, and without looking back, walked slowly out of the cemetery.

The house was quiet. She laughed to herself "No, it ain't quiet here; it's dead". Elaine sat at the kitchen table after dinner smoking a cigarette not looking at anything. She washed the dishes, dried them and put them away. She emptied the ceramic flower ashtray wiping away the grime making it look brand new, and then placed it back on the table. She climbed the stairs holding a glass of ginger-whiskey in one hand on her way to the bath.

She enjoyed the whiskey as she reclined in the tub surrounded with warm water. The corn on her foot was not hurting her as much as usual. She felt this was a good thing. After she toweled off she put on a clean night gown and gazed at the woman in the mirror, the one who was no longer a girl, and smiled.

Elaine remembered a dress she used to have, might still be in the closet she thought. She had never understood why Bob loved it so much until she asked him one night. He said "I could give two shits about that dress, I just love the way you make it look" He was a charmer sometimes, but his charm lay in the fact he wasn't attempting to charm. He said what he meant, and meant what he said. "God" she thought "I'm a lucky girl"

She was happy as she opened each capsule, pouring the powder into her empty whiskey glass. One after the other she emptied, remembering something Bob had said or done. The time they went on vacation and he apologized about the hotel room, wishing he could have afforded better. When he told his mother "Elaine was HIS wife period and end of damn story!" One capsule after the other, the white powder mixed with memory. When he got sick but said everything was going to be alright, even when he knew it wasn't. How when he was in pain…"He only worried about me", Elaine smiled, it was a sad, wistful, happy smile as she opened the last capsule emptying it into the glass.

Elaine brushed her teeth. She looked at the old lady staring at her from the mirror and said "Like it or not, I'm still a girl inside". She ran some warm water into the whiskey glass. She stirred it with the handle of her toothbrush until it was a milky white, and then turned off the light and walked into her bedroom. She arranged the pillows the way she liked them and crawled into her empty bed. She could hear the silence of her home. But in the same silence, she could also hear an echo…of times past.

She picked up the whiskey glass and drank everything in it experiencing a little shudder. She turned off the light on her nightstand; and an old lady reclined into her pillows feeling like the girl she used to be.

In the darkness she felt a single tear roll over her cheek making a warm path on her skin while passing between her earlobe and neck on its way to her pillow; and went to sleep.

The next morning did not come any earlier or later than it ever did, all of a sudden there it was. There was a faint scratch on the window screen, the wind pushing the old pine tree branch against the kitchen window. Only now, there was no one there to hear it.

THE BOOK SHOP

I think it is the smell draws me there,
And if not draws, certainly encourages me to loiter.
It has a simple tented green awning emblazoned with one word,
BOOKS

Located in the eighties on the upper west side,
It has been there next to forever
A magic shop if ever there was one,
Right here in my city, beckoning me;

There are shelves on the sidewalk right outside,
The front door
Filled with paperbacks,
Row upon row

Each one selling for a dollar a piece, pick one will ya?
Heck, pick two or three or four,
They are only a dollar a piece,
Something for everyone, just take a look.

But if you walk through that door,
You will be greeted by the greats.
Right there is Kipling, or do you enjoy
Something more contemporary?

Maybe the subject of sports?
An entire section to peruse,
Do you like music? Classic, pop or otherwise?
Take the stairs, there's a section at the top.

It is the smell I tell you,
A million or more volumes of knowledge near mildewed,
Right at your finger tips
Voices of the known and unknown whispering to you

So many words in so many volumes dating from
Forever gone
To right here and now,
The silent voices of the living and the dead

Calling to you from the shelves
Some so high you need a ladder to see them all
To hear them all
Each one begging you to feel them all

From a shelf their silent pleas from the grave;
"Hear me! This is what I thought!"
"This is what I felt! This is who I was!"
"Listen for a moment to my words, to my soul"

"I spoke them!" Cry the books, these words in dusty volumes,
"I uttered them for you, and we have never met"
"On this shelf I sit"
"Waiting only for an introduction to, you"

Oh how the heart was beating, in veins the blood flowing,
When words met paper, when thoughts became print,
So many speakers, so many slants of reason
Each one begging you for attention, for you to only turn a page.

I still say it is the smell…it overcomes me
When I plod through the shelves of souls,
Who reach out to humanity from time now and past,
Begging for my audience, pleading for my attention.

Only a book shop on the upper west side,
Smelling of mildew and age
Souls like ghosts reaching from the shelf may seem tragic,
But take a whiff, for what you smell is magic.

CHRISTMAS

There was blood in my mouth,
I knew it was Christmas again.

We always had a big tree, seemed like a thousand ornaments,
It was always pretty, Dad made sure of that,
He was good at the cosmetic stuff, always looked like happy family
In the house, with the wood heater burning the chill away

And always presents, so many presents,
Stacked and falling under the tree
Wrapped in colorful happy paper
With bows, and little name tags of the lucky recipients.

Back then my brother was still a baby of sorts,
Maybe walking a little, but still in diapers
Happy family,
As always viewed from the outside;

Oh but from the inside…
Colorful wrapping paper and a brightly lit angel
Sitting on the top of the tree,
Was always hiding my nightmare, my reality;

It is frightening now I look back on it,
Such a juxtaposition of emotions,
When everyone you know is happy in anticipation,
Anticipating Christmas bounty, happy family; and I the Fear

I could never say anything right with my father,
And if I said nothing at all,
He felt I was plotting against him, a bad little boy,
I was always posed; between hope and fright.

Of all the things taught not to trust,
Why did it have to be Christmas?
Is what a man reflects now, when looking back at the little boy,
Who stood helpless in a past best left forgotten.

I have never in my life adult life put rum in eggnog.
Because that was how it always started,
Maybe a cup of coffee and a cigarette for appearances,
But Christmas morning always began, for Dad, with eggnog.

And rum; I like rum, don't get me wrong,
But never will I put it in a glass of eggnog,
I don't think I could, because I don't want to remember,
Not even one of those past Decembers.

It is not the bruises one recalls, not really even the blood,
I think it was the light stinging of your scalp,
As you sit crying and hoping it will stop.
Hair is not something one should use to throw a little boy across a room
I think.

Christmas wrappings everywhere, all bright and cheerful,
Although the little boy is told how undeserving
He is of anything,
Anything at all

Children are surprisingly resilient, but they remember,
Everything they are told about themselves.
And they begin to believe, all of these things whether good or bad,
They will become if you are not careful, what they are told by their dad.

Survival is a good thing, you have to survive,
What's the choice?
It is simple, to live or to die
If all you wished for as a child was death; it's easy to be alive.

I'm not a fan of Christmas.
I put on a good show; sometimes I even have a tree,
But my father left me a gift,
I see Christmas as pain, I see it as guilt.

I have tears on my cheeks right now,
They're not for me though, I am all grown up.
I just wish I could take that little boy in my arms, and to hold him tight,
And say "Hey Kid, Merry Christmas, all of that never happened and you'll be alright"

There was blood in my mouth,
I knew it was Christmas…

GOOD MORNING

I reset my pocket watch (it runs slow),
Five minutes ahead this time,
It will be two weeks now,
Until I have to do it again.

I have the black shoe polish flaming,
(My shoes are a mess)
A pot of stew is on the stove bubbling,
Filling the kitchen with its spicy scents;

A pint in one hand, with the other reaching for a cigarette
I find myself
Thinking of you,
Who are an ocean and a five hour time difference away.

It is after one AM there,
I hope you are warm and sleeping,
Sleeping well,
A happy girl in slumbered dreams

So in this writing I suppose I would like you to know,
While you were sleeping,
You were awake in my heart,
And my heart crossed an ocean to caress your brow,

Desiring you to sleep in the black milk of peace,
To awake happy as birds singing in spring,
Awaken with the feeling of a young she-wolf, rolling in the grass after
the hunt,
Senses charged, hunger abated; excited for a new day.

Good Morning

WOLF THOUGHTS

There is no shiver, whilst standing in the cold wind
The night is no brighter than ever before
A crescent moon is solitary,
Surrounded by the same stars,
Promising no more than another evening;

And it would be ungrateful to ask for more,
I think.
But is MY thinking I consider in this,
Not that of the Wolf,
Whose thoughts I wish to fathom.

Proud and solitary beast,
Roaming, hunting, rolling,
Tongue lolling, through the grass,
What Wolf thoughts must they possess?
To be so alone, filled with Wolf contentedness,

Is what in my weak human frame, weak human brain I ponder,
For I too thrill in solitude, my Self an un-silent companion,
In my head chattering always it seems,
But in sleep I am running,
Through rolling hills of green, my silent wolf dreams.

Does a wolf snap and howl at the moon because,
He does not understand astral changes?
Or does he howl in the wind knowing full well,
The earth has never been new,
And Wolfish wisdom celebrates the infinite sameness of it all.

Unbridled freedom stretching,
Running into the night, the loam sinking beneath my flexing paws,
Stretching the wind itself in escape, lost in the chase

Hunting as the Wolf in dreams it seems I…but
Awake under a blanket filled with the same, self.

It is the Wolf dream I think…keeps me sane.

NIGHT AT THE OPERA

The multi-colored spot lights stretching from
The ornately decorated ceiling,
Looks from this vantage point as,
Sunlight breaking through dark clouds
Beams stretching to the tiny ocean which is the stage;

The Metropolitan Opera House in New York City
I sit high in a box,
In semi-darkness I lean to watch the performance,
While occasionally reclining to consider my socks
Red, gray, black argyles, the choice makes me happy.

In the orchestral tub far below I watch the conductor
In his intricate dance grasping in one hand a tiny wand,
The other turning a page sometimes,
His entire body demanding response
From musicians leaning, tweaking, blowing and strumming their magic.

The staging is magnificent, the costumes a marvel,
Through my ears this witchcraft enters my soul, and my soul gasps,
A gasp of recognition, of meeting centuries of other souls
Who sat in seats such as these, maybe considering their own socks,
While being filled with the majesty of the Opera; just like me.

Golden and crimson curtains as large as houses open a little or much,
Depending upon scene, upon a world created again; for a moment
I pull the flask from my inside jacket pocket, unscrewing the silver lid,
The odor of scotch whiskey invades this space,
I take my drink, sharp on the tongue, scent of leather, taste of lace.

I am a patron of the arts,
For many years have I attended the Opera and the Ballet.
It is a rare oxygen indeed, one inhales when in attendance,

The art of human talent all in one auditorium celebrating the past,
No silver screen, no recorded music, only flesh and blood at you cast.

This is where I am in love. Caught in a time balanced between eras,
The words of long dead writers, and music written from the grave;
It is exciting sharing a feeling with someone long gone from this place,
And any seat you sit in, allows you such grace
Lives never end, no matter the century; when the curtain opens, to begin again.

In the darkness I consider the shine on my shoes
Enjoying liberal draughts of the scotch I consume.
I hear the magical music touching my soul as I recline,
While in this little box of darkness in the Metropolitan Opera House in New York City,
I wish all the world for one moment, could at least once; feel like me.

A POET IT SEEMS

And here again I sit
Surrounded by ghostly words and spirits,
Apollo, are you truly dead?
Do Gods die, or travel to another plane?
I want to know! I want to know!

There was a time the only company
The poet who was alone would keep,
Was the scratching of a quill,
Whispering in the air around a candle flame,
Before he went to sleep;

These muses how they dance!
Through time, over ages sharing,
Words, thoughts, the deeds wrought
Affording no desire to follow a ticking clock
Quills were wings flying from a past and cannot be for naught!

I hear you! I hear you!
I feel your night as if it were my own,
Tiny sounds of quills scratching upon paper
Invade my mind and room and countenance,
In the corner of my eyes I see your shadow in vapored verse.

Were you lonely as you wrote?
Did you consider certain words as beauty?
Or did you consider beauty…
And struggle in lonely despair,
Attempting to fit which words might capture beauty's flair?

I want to know! I want to know!
Speak to me you ghosts of fleshly departed Gods of print,
You left me words! You left me only…

You
In gloriously complicated thoughts of your written truths;

Were there tears upon your cheeks as you scribbled?
Your bleeding heart with only ink onto a blank scroll
Did you gaze into the night wondering
What possessed you to strike in this once blank, now written space
Trying to reflect an unfeeling populace?

Oh, how I adore you scribes of old!
You were fearless in finding harbor from the storm of soul,
Brandishing the quill like a sword of light,
Illuminating both the future and the past,
Heartbreak, joy, sorrow and surcease the winds filling sails of your mast.

You are life! You are heart! You are Poets!
You give me breath where it was stolen,
You give me heart, when mine was broken,
You clutch my hands when there is no one else there,
How I adore thee, the echo of your forgotten care.

Apollo, hear my plea! You are not a forgotten deity!
Your muses they still sing the songs you taught them!
And they ring in the ears of those of us who still listen,
Amanda and I hear you clearly,
Amanda and I, we love you dearly!

Who would desire to be a poet?
For hearts must be broken in order to fill with joy again,
And a quill is a poor, but brilliant device
Lauding all good and bad and evil to know,
There is bravery in inking life, but a poet is forever alone.

PLATO'S MOON

The moon is full tonight, though blanketed with clouds
Spreading it's glow through folds of the cotton quilt of night.
I have always called it "Plato's Moon"
Because I know the moon I gaze at and consider,
Is the same one he watched so very long ago.

When I was seventeen years old, my girlfriends name was Tara,
We would sit on the dock by the lake at her grandfather's house,
Looking at this same moon, making promises to forever;
She said when she lived in Germany she called it "Mr. Moon"
Because it was the moon she spoke to about life.

She had been raped at a very young age, and trust was a difficult
Concept,
To her in many ways, but we would sit on the dock fishing
And kiss in the tender way only young lips will allow;
Under Mr. Moon, where all things past could fade upon our innocent
brow.

The clouds have parted and now there is Plato's Moon,
Glowing as brightly in the Manhattan sky,
As ever it did through the ages, through life's sometime gloom,
Plato's Moon I watch you feeling the haunt of ages,
Residing in the light you provide.

And I remember fishing on the dock with Tara one particular night.
We caught a long and thrashing water moccasin,
The snake splashing, twisting, furling, curling and unfurling,
Trying to escape,
We cut the line knowing death stained our hands; and wept for a snake.

Plato's Moon; I recall these times only when you are full,
Not the half, nor the crescent, but the whole.

My eyes search into the night filled with your brightness
Sharing yourself with everyone who has ever lived before,
Who gazed into your face feeling themselves reflected; a hoped sage.

I can't speak to the long dead Philosophers to ask what they meant,
Or to the Poet's, whose love of words were spent;
Reaching and hoping one person might read, and maybe understand,
How so many eyes have touched on a single moon over and over again,
I just call it "Plato's Moon", and think of it as a friend.

A full and shining remembrance not mine only, but all who've ever gazed,
From this earth into the star salted skies:
Saying to themselves "There has to be more to this than what resides in these eyes"
We are only of this world for a moment; a brief gaze into the stars,
And the moon, should remind us how small: yet how large we truly are.

From my window while smoking a cigarette I see the clouds have broken,
And there is Plato's Moon shining. Lighting up cotton candy clouds so bright,
Like white-gold; or simply, the moon.
All this while I sit here remembering all the times you've reflected,
The night's embrace, Plato's Moon...You.

LOVE SONG

She would tell me she loved me,
Often
And every time her voice would change;
Adding a lilt to the words,
But I could not feel it.

I would hear the words
Uttered in her sing-song way,
See them floating in front of me
Reaching to my ears,
But my heart never heard a thing.

Her eyes were green,
They were beautiful, but,
So was she.
Her eyes reminded me of the color produced,
By the sun shining through a pine bough in winter;

Often it seemed her hair,
Silky, soft and flowing,
Carried the scent of sunshine and prairie grass,
When a breeze would lift it to frame
Her too pretty face

"I love you"
She whispered in her sing-song way,
While we were sharing an umbrella in the rain,
Waiting for a light to change,
Making our way to the ballet;

I could hear the words,
Such special, meaningful words,
Dancing through the air to find me…

But her saying and my hearing, while sweet,
Means little without a heartbeat; delivered with no heat.

I think it was the sing-song way her voice changed,
The breathy sort of Marilyn Monroe delivery:
Made me suspect of
The truth, of the words,
Making my heart wary; and my soul a bit weary.

She would say "I love you"
And I never once felt it.
There was no heat.
No passion to halo the words,
Just "I love you" in whispered song.

There was always an air of duty about it;
As if she thought to herself:
"This is what I'm supposed to say,
So I will say it in my certain way
Doesn't everyone try to sweeten duty?"

I, for awhile replied in the same,
Without song or lilt
Because for awhile,
I had convinced myself,
I meant it.

I think the great poets could tell you,
Words mean little without the heat;
Of passion: to guide and frame them.
They are only words
If actions of the heart are unattached.

She used to say "I love you"
But I could never feel it.

She would say this because she felt she was supposed to,
And it showed.
I suppose things are easier to say…than ever do.

One bright summer day in Midtown Manhattan,
I told her it was over,
The We; We never were.
Her green eyes brimming with tears she said:
"I love you"

She said I love you,
This time with no lilt, no sing-song delivery,
For the first time, with heat;
The sky was blue and her eyes were green,
But it was too late.

EAST SIDE EVENING

We were sitting on the roof smoking cigarettes in the cold,
Brightly lit windows in buildings by, around, and towering over us,
Blotting out portions of the Manhattan sky
Each of us drinking a beer and laughing.
Thursday night on the Upper East Side.

We had already finished a small bottle of scotch,
It was keeping us warm
In the otherwise chilly night
My friend, he looked into the sky and muttered,
"I don't get it. Thirty years, and it was perfect"

I asked "What's that?"
My friend is an attorney and very young.
A youth I thought untouched by life's fickle intrusions
Of tragic infusions,
But I was wrong and could feel the fever of his crushed soul.

"They were perfect, PERFECT, for thirty years. They were perfect"
His parents you see, were getting a divorce.
I am of an age I sometimes forget what life does to youthful illusions,
He said again "They were a picture of perfection"
I didn't have the heart to tell him of how a picture; can be filled with
deception.

I made all of the sympathetic noises one does,
When in the presence of a heartbreak un-owned;
I knew there was nothing I could say
And little I could do, to ease his pain.
So I put out my smoke and said "Let's go inside for another drink"

It was warm in the apartment,
The walls were adorned with framed pictures of him and his lady.

He handsome, she beautiful, lot's of smiles,
He not ready to get married,
She of the opinion he was being contrary.

We drank and talked of youth and education,
Slowly moving from heartbreak to life;
(Which I knew was filled with enough)
But I wouldn't tell him that, he'll find out soon enough.
So we drank and laughed, and then left to go eat.

77th Street and York lit up, bars, restaurants, dry cleaners
Lining the sidewalks, casting neon shadows across your feet.
A liquor store by the bar we were going to caught my attention,
I said "Jason, you want a drink before we get to the bar?"
He said "We can't drink in there" and I laughed.

I purchased two tiny bottles of Jameson and we went back outside,
I handed him one under the streetlights.
We unscrewed the little metal caps and made a toast,
On a sidewalk in the night in New York City we drank,
I told Jason to never forget "Manhattan IS your bar"

We walked into the pub flush with whiskey and ready for food,
When sitting on barstools he asked:
"What do you want to eat?"
I looked at the hardwood floors, listened to the clack from the billiard
table and replied:
"Let's make it something awful and delicious"

The barmaid was a tall blonde and not a kid,
When she took our orders I found out she was from Louisiana and her
name was Lana,
I said "Like Lana Turner?" she smiled and nodded.
I almost fell in love, but drank some more beer instead.
She sashayed to the other end of the bar like she was in a blue-jeans

commercial.

There was a blonde and a brunette girl sitting near us,
Tight green dress on the blonde, a violet low cut blouse on the other,
I watched them for a moment, enjoyed their womanly grace
I remarked to Jason how they made me wish I were younger,
He told me they make him wish he were single; or at least sneakier.

We had spicy chicken parts and dipped them in creamy sauces,
As if proclaiming to the Gods of health,
For this evening, no thank you, we will take our chances,
But in the morrow we promise,
To maybe have a salad; and chewed our food to the rhythm of a loud
juke box.

I spied my reflection in the mirror behind the bar,
The place I used to see a much younger me staring back,
My hair too long, my scarf askew,
But still a beer in my hand after all these years,
I smiled at him and he smiled back at me.

The music was loud and the air filled with drunken laughter,
The beer was cold and the whiskey warm;
On this blue globe we spun, not caring about:
The heartbreaks of the day, or the pain, or uninvited sorrow,
We were drunk as lords ignoring any threat of tomorrow.
Jason's girlfriend unexpectedly joined us;
Took one look at her love and rolled her eyes like only a beautiful wom-
an can,
Jarring memories of a younger me,
When I was being reckless, happy and unaware,
Of the eyes rolling at me; a reminder time is a treacherous lover.

The evening was coming to an end and I thought,
This is the sort of day one should hope for,

The kind of day blurs into the night,
Where friendship, silliness and intoxicated talk,
Breathes life into your very soul, a day you could call a ride.

We parted on the sidewalk,
Shaking hands and promising to soon do it again,
The sloppy intoxicated brotherhood of drink
Well meaning and avoiding how no one knows,
To what place nights like these go.

Drunkenly I began walking, looking for a bus stop, a way home
Three streets and I find an avenue to pause and wait.
A German man asked me if a bus here would get him uptown,
I told him "Yes, if one should ever show"
It was late and I was drunk and a long way from home.

His friend joined us and I was introduced to another name I forgot im-
mediately,
I mentioned a cab would only cost them ten bucks or so,
He said: "Ah, but zis ees moneys better to spend on zee beer"
They walked away as we laughed together,
I could hear the echoes of their mirth bouncing off glass windows as
they left.

The bus never showed, so I looked at my shoes and decided to walk,
And walk, and walk, and walk.
I was still on 77th Street, forgetting it bisects into Central Park
I was on the East Side, trying to get to the West Side,
Well fuck.

Central Park was cloaked in darkness spread before me as far as I could
see,
To get across I would have to walk south to 59th Street,
Or north to 96th,
Either way was long, I considered as I peered into the darkness of the

park;
Or conversely, I could walk through the middle, at one AM, which
would be dumb.

Of course I went with dumb, because when I'm drunk I'm smart.
I clamped my awful looking silver headphones onto my head,
Cranked up the music loud enough to cover the sensible unease,
A reasonable human feels about embarking upon the stupid,
And resolutely, with AC/DC blasting into my cranium, strode into the
park.

I walked some on the street, and some on the paths.
I ignored the incredulous stares from various statues,
Seemingly asking me what exactly in the hell I was doing.
I mentally told them to mind their own business,
Then chided myself for speaking to inanimate history

The dark forest, lined and dotted with standing lamps,
Of the type used to burn gas in a different age
Now the white glow of electricity
Instead of the lonely yellow flicker of flame used to burn,
In the same sort of globes so long ago in the past

No other soul did I see in my self imposed march stirring,
No car, nor carriage to dodge in my path,
Walking through Central Park in the dead of early morning
Testing fate, in my search for the West Side,
Walking and telling myself my shadow was nothing to fear.

I was walking past a hillock dotted with giant gray stones,
Guarded by huge trees spreading their boughs like blankets in the air;
When in my ears from my device played a piece by Bizet,
I climbed the hill looking around tree trunks for the homeless denizens,
Or the wolves I suppose, knowing inside myself I was only looking at
my own fear.

After finding no one or nothing, I stood looking into the semi-darkness;
Through the trees I could see buildings reaching to the sky,
The bright-lit city surrounding the park,
Out of reach of my feet,
But in the realm of my eyes, the distant Camelot waiting, for my return;

I fumbled with the ipod, restarting Bizet, and turned the volume to high.
An orchestra exploded into my ears, filling my soul past the darkness where I stood.
I inhaled the night. I felt the grass beneath my shoes spongy and damp,
And alone beneath the trees, surrounded by the great gray stones,
I threw my arms into the air and conducted an orchestra seen only by me.

I waggled my fingers and violins sprang to life,
I swanned my hands to hear the clarinets twinkle.
A great cymbal responded to my grasped fist!
I stood on a hill in Central Park in the dark twisting and turning with delight,
Conducting my orchestra into the night, and for one tiny moment; felt like a God!

The music stopped.
Damp darkness surrounded me and my breath was a plume before my eyes,
I laughed heartily to myself,
Because for one tiny moment in my tiny life I thought,
I was Apollo standing on earth; and then called myself a silly bastard.

I walked down the hill to another path,
Lining the path were benches, side by side, end to end,
I thought they looked guilty sitting there with purpose un-served,
A cold patina of condensation on their boards,
Wishing someone, anyone, would come and sit.

On another hill I noticed, reaching into the sky,
A great black obelisk, seeking to penetrate the heavens
I walked up this hill hopping over a small wrought iron fence,
To read a plaque saying this was transported from Egypt
I leaned placing my hand against the cold stone to be transported some-
where else myself.

I began walking again,
And walking, and walking, and walking,
In the distance I saw the lights of a street,
The west side at last!
Into the street I meandered to find it was Lexington.

Damnit! I had walked a circle in the park and still,
Was on the east side far from home,
Too stubborn to hail a taxi
I searched for a subway kiosk,
Knowing far from over, was my little roam.

I found the six train, and walked resolutely down the stairs,
To wait five minutes for the east side train,
To take me to Grand Central Station,
To again wait,
For the seven to take me to Times Square

People on the subway in New York are always interesting to notice,
But at two AM, it gets special.
There was a man sitting on the hard blue plastic seat,
His chin on his chest, obviously asleep,
I looked a bit closer and thought "Jesus! What a set of tits on this guy"

Upon closer inspection, I saw the sleeves of his pullover shirt were
empty,
And dangling at his sides,

He had tucked his arms inside his shirt and it looked as if he needed a
bra,
And then I saw the gash on his forehead not quite seeping blood,
And knew he'd had a rough night.

We pulled into Grand Central, where in order to get to the seven train,
You ride a very long escalator into the bowels of the city
Where far below you wait for the train
That at this hour, its coming and goings,
Are far from reliable;

In my silver headphones I listened to Guns and Roses,
Sing to me of November Rain
And all around me were employees of the transit authority spraying
down,
Everything
With high pressure hoses spraying hard mists of water like a wet drag-
ons breath.

And they dressed with goggles and masks and protective clothing,
I had walked into the midst of the morning aliens,
Astronauts of duty and night, cleaning passages,
Knowing morning will not remember,
The duty of their labor: the thankless legacy of those who clean the
filth, of a city.

So I rode the escalator up from the depths,
This night had been made for walking
And Times Square was not so far away.
I passed a young black girl sitting on the floor crying,
Her clothes dirty, her life a two AM nightmare in Grand Central Station.

The lights are still bright in the early, early morning in Manhattan,
I walked down 42nd street by the library and Bryant Park,
There was a crowd of people wandering the streets,

I looked at my pocket watch and wondered,
What they were doing out at this hour…and then thought the same of
myself.

The sun never goes down in Times Square,
This always surprises me when I find myself there in the wee hours.
I see the cops walking with lackadaisical purpose to no where,
The disenfranchised picking up cigarette butts,
Begging passerby for a light;

It has become late, and I am tired and still a bit drunk,
When I walk down the steps to board a west side train
By the candy seller is a tall police officer reading a newspaper,
His shorter partner standing at his shoulder looking at the page,
Both in NYPD blue, wearing hard billed hats with pistols on their sides.

The wait for the One train is horrible.
So I catch the Two to 96th street,
Feeling as if motion is commotion and it is the direction of home.
Across from me sits a beautiful girl in a white jacket,
Wearing black, scuffed velvet boots reaching to her knees;

Her chin rests on an alabaster fist,
Eyes closed,
Fake eyelashes sweeping,
Just below her eyes,
She does not open them as she sways with the movement of the train.

I don't stare, because it would be rude,
But I can't help but to notice how pretty she is,
And in the late night I recall holding hands with girls as pretty as she
Before time came to visit and tell me,
Youth was truly a lovely pastime taken for granted.

An older me also wondered if she were as pretty a person,

As she is a woman,
Things I never thought of in my youth.
She swayed with the movement of the train all the way to 96th street.
Where we both disembarked

I watched her walk away in the tunnel sending her a silent wish,
Life would be kind,
That she would always be beautiful;
And there would come a time in her life,
She would not be on a train at three o'clock in the morning.

The digital sign told me it would be eleven minutes before my train,
Pulled into this station to carry me home;
I gazed into the dirty tracks wondering,
Why so many ink pens were littered,
And a scarf much like my own was draped in discard or loss.

Time in waiting will attack you with memories,
And Gizel came to mind. A beautiful woman who loved me once,
It struck me like lightening this memory, doubling my psyche over in
pain,
Making me know time refuses to tick when you want it to go faster,
So you may have a moment to reflect on regret and disaster.

The train came barreling down the track to stop in front of me,
Not knowing the heartbreak,
It gave me in my waiting;
For it's untimely arrival,
But I boarded with a sigh, for home was five stops in the future.

I walked through the door of my apartment,
The cat scrutinizing me from his carpeted perch,
I patted his head relieved to see him,
Relieved the evening was over and I was finally on the west side alone;
I realized…whiskey and a good pair of shoes will always get you home.

SPRING

I felt it. I know I did. The lightest kiss imprint on my arm,
The sensation of heat not unlike some one's lips pressed
Upon me: Warmth upon my brow, the memory of a warm kiss now.

I felt it, I know I did.
From my window where I sat smoking a cigarette into the morning,
And then later walking to the bathroom blinded by Spring sun.

It was a breeze blowing smoke back into my face with a promise,
Winter has receded to no longer a maybe
It will snow, sleet, or hinder the trees from turning green.

It is a fickle lover this season,
Willing to hold your hand for a moment whilst singing with joy,
Then turn on you with a cold reminder tomorrow may change.

I love this season because I love the symphony,
Spring is the season of music. It is violins and cymbals,
Teasing with the sun and a warm breeze: Nature the conductor of
whims;

Begging and reaching for you to remember to right now,
To right this very moment and now,
You have the music, sing again!

The sun now a delicate kiss,
Lips pressed upon your brow, arms and face,
Begging you to remember last year's embrace.

It is said the seasons change but this I deny,
For year after year the seasons reach to us the same,
That we see them differently means only we have changed.

What is Spring to a child?
But hope for Summer?
And here we are again wearing the hope of a child.

Hoping the new sun will again provide the greenery
We pay no attention to, as if it were never there
Every Spring we have ever lived through.

Spring is memory renewed; of love forgotten until now,
The Now being the kiss of the sun desired,
Which Spring withholds and gives unremittingly.

Over and over again from day to day is Spring a tease to the senses,
One day a kiss, another only the memory of
A kiss hoped for again.

All of our loves, those now and forgotten or hoped for,
Find reflection in the season of Spring,
For this is the time we for one tiny moment, remember how to love
again.

HEARTS AND HAIR

Ah man. That was not a memory I needed.
This girl with the really long hair standing in front of me,
It was cascading down her back
Shiny and sleek and beautiful,
Like a silken waterfall.

I saw her hair and remembered, a pink hair brush,
A foam handle, spindled black tines in a half-sphere.
I could recall the touch of the brush handle in my hand,
Spongy in my grip as I brushed her long blonde hair,
One hand with the brush, the other following catching static;

She would sit on the floor, with me on the couch,
Her watching the television, me brushing her hair
I can't watch television, it makes me crazy,
I prefer books.
But I could brush her hair, while she enjoyed her stories.

Her hair was long…and blonde and lush.
With the right stroke of the brush, in the right light,
I could see sparkles of static electricity muted and dim
Biting at my fingers lightly like minnows in a pond,
I could get lost in that hair, and never want to be found.

Late at night when her programs were finished,
We would make love before the glowing screen
The volume muted, only soft sounds of gentle passion,
Coming from us, to us; the Us of the private us.
Sighs, exclamations, a fast breathy exhalation of approval; love sounds.

She had the longest, blondest, silkiest hair.
In moments of passion it would be wrapped around my fist,
In moments of repose, draped across my chest,

In my dreams I remember how it smelled,
Of cigarette smoke and honeysuckle;

She would on a moment laugh for no reason,
And I felt as if my heart would explode.
Because trumpets blown by angels from on high,
Could not make notes of music filling my ears,
Sound as lovely or perfect. Silver in my heart was her laughter.

Late nights in Manhattan we would prowl in dark establishments,
Me with my scotch and water,
Her with chardonnay shimmering in stemmed crystal glasses.
Daring the evenings to end without us,
And leave together in yellow taxis driven by men wearing turbans.

No matter where we were, or how she dressed,
Or how long we were there, or what jacket I wore,
Or when we left or where we went;
The next day or the next hour, the moment she was gone:
On my person I would find a strand of long blonde hair somewhere.

She began taking pills,
I don't know what they were.
But I knew after an hour,
She was no longer the Her,
The Her I knew.

The clock ticked, because it refuses to stop,
Even if you need it to, if only to fit
The feelings stuck in a time past before, to make them stay,
The very next tick, treacherous ticking, will not relent;
Even if you are losing something, and want it for one second to quit

To give you time to think, figure things out. Fix it dammit!
Because the long blonde hair you have brushed,

Held in your fist and had draped across your chest;
Had grown in length, managed to reach the protected part,
This silken hair went and wrapped around my heart.

Ah man. That was not a memory I needed.
The girl with the really long hair standing in front of me,
Cascading down her back
Like a silken waterfall,
Who knew hair could break a heart?

CRUSHED FLOWERS

It was late afternoon I think, many years ago,
On the west side, 51st street and 9th avenue,
Inside a small round green metal trash can,
A phalanx of broken stems,
And crushed flowers spilling from its top

Little more than a cursory glance I gave it as payment
For passing by;
Summer in Manhattan the senses are filled,
With the comings and goings of a multitude;
A multitude of sensations, odors, and people.

In the City; one is always in a hurry; going to their own wherever;
You see a million things in a single glance,
Rarely noticing anything at all
In this race to nowhere,
The moment deems important.

Snapping pictures of everything
Is how your brain stays busy,
Putting them in a file you are not aware of,
Until in a moment of repose you receive a flash,
Of a second; an impression, a forgotten picture of the past.

The crushed petals were blue with a yellow stain.
They looked soft, pliable and beautiful;
But with crushed drooping heads,
Atop the broken green stems,
Still littered with not yet browning leaves

I must have looked for a longer time than I recall,
For this picture to have stuck in my mind;
Unbidden recollection of crushed flowers in my head,

Blue as the twilight sky over an ocean,
A stain of yellow suggesting the departing sun:

What made me thing of them? Why this forgotten image?
What was I thinking of, brought them to my imagination?
And before I sip the wine from this glass,
Wine red as the blood of forgotten souls departed;
I know in full body realization, the revelation, which is reflective of my dreams.

Tonight I found a tiny strip of pictures, of two.
They were in my Grandfathers wallet,
Stored in a chest drawer, a treasure I had forgotten.
There I was, no more than five years old sitting in his lap,
The flash of the camera lighting his eye glasses;

The sort of pictures you used to get sitting in a booth,
After closing a curtain
For two warm quarters dug out of your pocket.
They were black and white: and forever was captured,
On this tiny strip of photos, quaint in time, then lost in the ether;

That time produces. We grow up and forget so many things,
We spend our time working to buy or rent or support,
What started out as dreams became a day to day chase,
Chasing after what we were taught to want, to achieve.
We sometimes work for everything but those original dreams.

Ah! Dreams! And there it is,
Why my brain recorded, in order to someday remind me;
Giving up is worse than forgetting:
Long lost pictures, reminding of love and what that love would desire,
Because one should never think of their dreams as crushed flowers...

Thank you Pawpaw

CHAIN IN WIND, SHACKLE OF LOVE

It is in the breeze my Darling; I find thee so often.
Whether summer soft; or winter damned,
You cannot hide. For the wind is honest,
It desires as much as I; for thee to rest at my side.

Tears of centuries may stain our faces,
Though matted the tracks they leave, I will find you.
Chain in wind…links, one after one,
Ensuring though times parted, I shall find thee again.

My Darling, I know you are there; and where,
As a wild animal I find your scent;
In the wind, the honest and truthful breeze,
I beg of thee, to stop running from this destiny.

We are of one. Our One is eternal, immortal,
The price paid. Over and over the ledger is in black
No purse of shame. No voice abhorring from below or above
To crack…dismantle or break; these shackles of love.

It was the silence, I think, Amanda; which overwhelmed me.
There are storms in the air making the neighborhood quiet,
No sirens softly (or harshly), snaking through the window,
When I noticed the stillness of my kitchen;
When I realized I was alone.

I had been listening to an Artist's recording,
A song he wrote and sang.
I never met the young man,
But as life gives you irony and soothe,
I remembered the funeral home.

Today is his birthday.
If it makes a difference at all to the departed
He would have been thirty two.
Yet now he is gone, leaving only;
The love of those who knew him, and a song or two

Recorded for someone like me to find and listen to.
I sat in the silence, not realizing how silent it was.
Because a moment before he was singing,
Into the silence,
Making it whole…

He was the brother of a close friend.
I should say "is" because "was" is a mistreatment;
For he has never left the many hearts,
He lives in memory,
And will never depart.

I don't think we leave too many things,
Having a real value…an honest touch;
But if we can leave,

Tears on another's face;
We have left love; which there is never enough.

In the silence of my kitchen,
I was overwhelmed
With the voice of a young man reaching from the grave;
Telling me there is even hope in sorrow. And to always remember,
Live for tomorrow.

LOVE

I hazard in mentioning, this word love; I'm not sure
Letters of the word only four,
Meaning what?
Yet, written of over the ages.

Love; what is this thing? This idea, this revelation
But a word;
Wherein thought arises, to the warm lights of the stage,
The one we stand upon, begging to worship or be worshipped.

It is Love, makes the heart patter; the blood heat.
In the places letters do not matter,
It is where we keep our sighs;
All close to our chests, for fear of…of.

We stand alone in our Love,
In our Loves, for all our lives we stand;
Alone
We stand singular in a pool of hope begging a return;

Of Love
And every night in the arms of another we are alone,
With the Love;
We are wishing returns, to us; in the same strength.

Kisses sweet walking in time, hoping only to keep step
Marching towards the end, marching…
In lock-step we pray;
To Love.

Love of our mates, love of our family; love of…
Our Love;
For the mirror's kindness, lasts only so long,

And the reflection will surely in time, account for our wrongs.

The child's small hand held in ours,
The warmth of their innocence we feel soaking into our;
Into our past…our skin
While we gaze into the eyes of the untouched

Untouched by the fickleness life will surely share,
Unencumbered of memories to keep them awake,
Allowed to sleep in the silent comfort of Love, knowing nothing else,
And this…is Love.
Going to sleep in Love,
Not even knowing what Love is.
Waking up in Love;
In the joy of another day

Is more simple than one would imagine.
We just close our eyes, and remember when;
Our Love felt natural, was as normal as the sky,
And we were able to reflect this, eye to eye…

I cried into the night,
And the night heard;
Until I could cry no more,
And became the night,
And found,
Night.
For all the illusions pressed,
Cannot hide from the darkness,
And all of light cannot plumb,
The Night.
All religion was built for fear of the dark,
To give faith;
Hope,
When the howling turns ones bones to water,
And the fear, the fright,
Comes visiting,
In the Night.
Darkness is the velvet behind closed eyes,
But the Night's darkness intrudes when they are open,
And Night,
King Night burrows into the soul.
I cried into the night,
And the Night heard,
Until I could cry no more,
And became the Night,
And found;
Night.

INTRODUCTION TO PIECES SELECTED BY AMANDA

Well, I sincerely hope you enjoyed the first part of the book, because I will be quite honest with you, I sincerely enjoyed writing it. Although to tell you the truth, when I was writing those pieces, I never considered putting them in print. As I mentioned before, I was scribbling for Amanda's amusement. Who knew I would end up scribbling so much? With the exception of the last piece "Night", I did indeed write all the works in From December to July in said time period. "Night", I wrote a couple of weeks ago to Amanda using my iphone, fully in my cups, somewhere around the area of four AM. After I sent it to her she said she liked it, so I told her I would cheat it into the book. Now I feel all virtuous for telling you the truth should you care. When I first started considering this as a book, I did not tell Amanda, I just looked at the work asking myself if there was enough to make a decent volume. There was enough, but I wondered if I were going approach Neal, my publisher, shouldn't I have a large enough work to appease his publishing sensibilities? So, being the sneak I am, I started sending pieces I had written over the last twenty five years or so to Amanda to ask her what she thought of them. Now I am not a fool, I have no doubt she tired of my assault of prose into her inbox, so things she did not comment on, I left out. See? Sneaky. Anyway, after a few months of this I shared with her the idea for the book, and now, in your hands, rests said book. Her approval is stamped upon each and every thing you read, the only difference of the two parts is from December to July was written specifically to amuse her; everything afterward is an anthology of sorts from my scribbles over the years. It begins with short stories, a format which I truly enjoy writing in. Finding the emotion of a specific character and then in a short time getting to know them, and sharing their souls with the reader is a very rewarding experience in my opinion. I hope you enjoy them. The quiet acceptance of circumstance Carl wears, to the frustration of Morton. The excitement of youth Brandon is not even aware of, and in White Squall, realizing one can love a parent for all their mystery. I am now going to put a disclaimer of sorts on the short story "Sheila's Dead". I wrote it specifically for a small gothic magazine in

New Jersey in 2002 or so. I recall lighting candles around the kitchen table, opening a large bottle of cognac, cranking up some Marilyn Manson on the stereo, and saying into my inner-soul, "Lets write something as absolutely horrible as has ever been done, and then make it worse". Hence the story Sheila's Dead. I do not encourage you to read it if you have a weak constitution as I promise you it will offend sensibilities you were not aware you possessed. So, that being said, if you decide to read it and then are ticked off at me, don't say I didn't warn you.

After short stories comes poetry. I broke it into three categories: *Of Alabama, of Home*. *Of Love or Something Like It*; and *Life and its Happenings*. I think this explains them for what they are. Except for the fact, they are quite simply, ruminations of my soul. A quill is a wondrous and exciting thing to hold in ones hand, it truly is your soul. And now, not only Amanda, but you; are holding mine. Enjoy.

The boy sat transfixed. He had been sitting there for awhile. He was at the very edge of a gravel road, he was sitting cross-legged just like the Indians he had seen on the television. He did not feel like an Indian. He did not know what he felt like, although he often wondered how he was *supposed* to feel.

Ten to twelve feet in front of him there was a broken power line draped over the road. The end of it was a melted rubber and plastic gaping maw filled with broken wiring resembling teeth. It hissed and sputtered, throwing showers of blue sparks along its path. The power line having been severed from its conduit was now arcing all over the place searching for a connection.

The boy did not know this. He was enjoying watching the line snake around tossing hissing sparks. It was quiet as a mausoleum except for the whoosh, hiss, of the electric line pitching on the ground. The gravel road was lined with woods, creating a green, leafy canopy over the boy and his show. In either direction the road stretched until it became the shadow of the towering trees lining it created. The boy watched the broken power line skitter around in front of him. It reminded him of the bottle rockets he launched on the fourth of July. He thought it was neat.

The boy's name was Carl, short for Carlson. Carlson was his Grandfather on his Father's side of the family's name. His Father insisted he be named after a man Carl would never have the opportunity to meet, being as his Grandfather died shortly after Carl was born. This was not what Carl was thinking of at the moment. Carl was watching the big black power line float ghost-like, dipping and rising, he could hear the gravel crunch together as the heavy line dragged itself back and forth over the surface of the road. Occasionally the fiery blue white head of the electrical line would snap at the ground creating a small intense explosion; then magically levitate, twisting it's melted sparkling head in one direction and then the other. Almost as if searching, or hoping, for something to bite. Carl watched wondering.

Carl spent much of his time thinking, wondering. He would at times invent complete lives in his mind. Always lives unlike his own. Carl at one time liked to talk, but increasingly when he spoke at home, his Father would slap him and tell him to shut his stupid mouth before he got it shut for him. Therefore Carl frequently became lost in his own thoughts. No one ever slapped him when he was thinking, so Carl figured thinking must be OK. Carl spent a lot of his time thinking. He spent a lot of his time dreaming.

The severed power line struck the ground snake-quick with a kazapp!! Then sprung four feet into the air in an arcing motion creating a small electric blue rainbow, the air reeked of burnt ozone. The line settled down into a gentle whipping motion, swaying back and forth, a solitary dance, a hypnotic mindless waltz. The boy did not cringe. He did not budge an inch. Displayed on his face was a tiny smile. Carl was thinking.

Carl did not have any brothers or sisters. His Father was fond of saying one extra worthless mouth to feed was ample enough. When Carl's Father said this, usually when he was drunk or rapidly progressing in that direction; Carl's Mom would timidly look down towards the ground; as if she were inspecting the laces on her shoes. Carl's Mother did not say much either. Carl guessed she spent a lot of time thinking too, but he never asked.

Carl and his Mother were like bedraggled survivors of a shipwreck. Afloat together on a tiny life boat, Carl's Father was the ocean. Carl and his Mother knew there would be no rescuers out searching for them. They knew theirs was a duty of resignation. They would weather the storms and the sunny days, but in the end, the ocean would be the victor. The ocean was bigger than both of them, and hope was an elusive mirage, to be seen briefly but never relied upon. Such was their lot in life, such was their acceptance.

Carl watched the sparkling end of the magic electric line spit fire and writhe around like a dying eel. He traced with his eyes, from the ground up to where the line had once been attached to a gray transformer perched upon a gigantically tall round shaft. The gray transformer was smudged with black streaks from where the lightning had left its legacy; where Nature violently merged for an instant with the ideals of man. For the moment it would be man who lost. A small battle for sure, but the war would rage on. And in time, Nature will surely reclaim it's own. Time. Carl thought of this for a moment, and then closed his eyes.

Carl remembered a day long ago. To a child, long ago could be anywhere from a week to a year. Such is how time works for children. Carl and his parents were sitting in the living room of their home, watching television. The show was Wild Kingdom. On this particular program the theme was Birth in the Wild. Carl's Father had not been drinking this day, so Carl was reasonably comfortable in the company of his parents. He was also pleased to be able to feel this way. It was a sensation he was not accustomed to.

On the television screen there was a panoramic scene of some exotic country side in Africa or some other fantastic place. The camera zoomed in on what looked to be an antelope or deer of sorts. The narrator's voice, tinged romantically with a proper Englishman's accent, was describing the life of this foreign creature. He droned on of the predators it avoided in its daily existence. He spoke of the vegetation required for its diet; he spoke generally of its lifestyle in the wild. Carl was fascinated. He enjoyed this type of program. He was all of the time dreaming of far off incredible places in the world and what type of animals and people lived there. From his imagination to the television screen, he was comfortably in an element of familiarity.

Carl's Mother and Father were sitting on the couch. Carl was sitting on the floor with his legs bent up, holding his arms around his knees, a picture of domesticity. The

Narrator of the program announced the antelope was about to experience the miracle of birth. With rapt attention Carl watched as the creature began the process. From the hind quarters of the straining beast emerged wet little hooves, which quickly became fragile little legs and a torso slick with mucous. Inches at a time slid this tiny creature from the shuddering animal. Then the small head of the fawn appeared as it fell to the ground. With the grandest of struggles the new baby fought to get to its feet. All in all, it was a miracle to behold.

Carl glanced over to his Father and quite innocently said, "Daddy, did that baby fall out of his Momma's butt?" The ensuing explosion would be something Carl would both never forget, and equally never understand. His Father grabbed him by his hair and screamed "BOY, I'LL NOT HAVE THAT KIND OF TRASH TALK IN THIS HOUSE!!" Carl's Mother screamed "LET HIM BE! THE BOY WAS JUST CURIOUS" as Carl's Father dragged him by the hair from the living room into the boy's bedroom. His Father tossed him by his hair onto the bed where he sprawled out like a broken doll. By this time Carl was not only terrified, but was also seeing stars from having his scalp nearly yanked off. Tears were running down Carl's cheeks and he was trembling all over. The fear was so intense it seeped into his tiny seven year old soul and became a chattering banshee threatening to eat him alive.

Carl's Father meanwhile was rummaging through the boy's closet, mumbling profanities about children having no respect and if *his* Father were alive to hear this crap what would happen; and God only knows what else was passing through his clenched teeth and pursed lips. Carl lie on the bed whimpering how sorry he was, when his Father discovered the object he was searching for, there in the corner of the closet leaned a toy spear, replete with a rubber arrow head and feathers on the end of the shaft. The shaft was a bamboo stick varnished a dark brown. It was about four and a half feet long.

His Father grasped the toy and then turned to face Carl. Carl saw the fervent zealots gleam in the eyes of his Father, a look he had seen many times in the past; a look which would haunt his dreams for more years than he could possibly imagine, a look chilling him to his very bones.

His Father walked over to the bed, once again grabbed Carl by his hair, and threw him across the small room and into the wall. Carl crumpled to the floor. Through tear bleary eyes the boy saw the silhouette of his Mother standing in the door way, her arms folded, tears streaming down her cheeks from behind her eye glasses. All Carl could think was "Don't cry Mommy, please don't cry".   Then the beating began.

His Father was screaming "I'LL NOT RAISE A FILTHY MOUTHED LITTLE HEATHEN IN THIS HOUSE! I WILL NOT HAVE IT!!! Carl could feel the bamboo shaft hitting his legs and his back. He would try to squirm away and his Father would grab him by his little arm and yell "YOU'RE NOT GOING ANYWHERE YET!!" The pain was sharp and it came in streaks and waves, it seemed to sting and burn at the same time. The pain enveloped Carl until he was nothing but pain. His Father kept on and on, swinging and whacking, his arm would rise and strike the child, then his arm drew over and back hitting from a different angle, over and over and over again until Carl could not even cry because his throat had became so dry. Then, seemingly as quickly as it started; it stopped. Carl's Father had a confused look on his face. He stared down at his trembling and shaking child. He then looked at the toy turned disciplinary weapon in his hand. He threw down the toy and walked out of the room. Carl's little heart was beating so fast he was dizzy. His back and legs felt scorched. He was trembling. In some dark corner of his mind he was glad it was over; but already dreading the next time.

Carl opened his eyes just as the electric line whipped past his face. He felt the shift of his hair from the force of its passing. He felt the tingling on his cheeks where electric particles brushed him. He could smell the tarry burnt rubber smell of the damaged line. The black line snaked to the middle of the road and lay there like a wounded serpent. Twitch and lie still. Shift and twitch again, the hiss of burning electricity in the air, the silence of the woods; the heartbeat of a little boy.

Carl leaned back a little, looked around, and wondered if anyone was going to come and fix the toppled electric line. He thought maybe who ever it was who fixed electric lines might have kids and might want to introduce them to Carl. Carl would like to make some friends. Actually, Carl would have been happy with one friend, anyone.

Carl looked over at the fallen electric line. It was for the moment lying dormant. Carl looked at the ground between his knees. He took the flat of his palm and spread gravel and sand over to one side, making a clear spot of dirt, a chalk board on the road. With his index finger he began drawing circles. He would draw one, wipe it away. He would draw one; and then draw another through it. Wipe it away. He drew a bunch of little circles and wiped them away. He drew a tic-tac-toe grid, and thought of his Mom.

Carl loved his Momma. She would lay in bed with him and tell him stories of when she was a little girl, and she would let him ask all the questions he wanted to until he went to sleep. In the mornings when Carl woke up, he could smell the coffee and bacon, could hear the sizzle of the eggs his Mom was frying in a skillet in the kitchen. Carl would lie in his bed until his Father left for work, then get up to go see his Momma. He never told her how many times he heard his Father say "the lazy little bastard won't even get up to eat" Carl didn't care. When he went into the kitchen his Momma would always smile and say "hello sleepy head, the bed bugs didn't bite did they?" Carl would giggle and shake his head no. He would then crawl up onto one of the big kitchen chairs and his mom would bring him a glass of cold milk. He loved her smile, he loved her.

Carl looked at the tic-tac-toe grid he drew in the sand. He glanced over to the power line in the middle of the road, it was quiet this moment. He remembered when his Momma taught him how to play tic-tac-toe. She took a piece of ruled paper and a pen, with her delicate hands she drew two lines long ways, and then crossed through those lines with two lines up and down. She now had a small grid made up of nine boxes. She then scrawled an X in the middle box. She told him you only used Xs and Os in this game. She showed him how you win by getting three of your marks in a row. He could do this either across the grid, straight up and down, or even diagonally. She taught him how to make his mark, how to block his opponent, and how to win. He watched her lips as she explained it. He watched her hands as she showed him. He was enthralled. He must have the smartest Mom in the world.

That day he could not wait for his Father to get home from work to show him the new game Momma taught him. He wanted to show his Dad he learned something new. Carl wanted his Father to be proud of him. Carl's Father came in at his usual time. Went straight to the refrigerator and got a beer, and sat down at the kitchen table. Carl came in and told his Father about the game his Mom taught him. Carl very carefully drew the tic-tac-toe grid on a sheet of paper and asked his Father if he would like to play. Carl's Father looked at him and said "Sure, why not?" His Father beat him at the game several times, told him how stupid he was, and finally told him to come back and challenge the old man again when he thought he was ready for another ass whipping. Carl dutifully said "Yes Sir", gathered the pen and papers they were playing on, and went to his room. He did not cry.

Carl wiped the tic-tac-toe grid away and began to draw circles again. He really didn't like tic-tac-toe anyway. He heard a hiss, looked up and watched the power line lift off of the ground again. It rose two feet or so, weakly swayed back and forth for a moment, then fell dead on the road. It was no longer sputtering. Carl guessed someone was fixing it now. Carl leaned over and using his hands he pushed himself off of the ground. When he was standing he brushed the dust and dirt from the backside of his jeans with his palms. He could feel the grit in the palms of his hands and in the webbing between his fingers. He brushed his hands brusquely together with a motion which did not look entirely unlike clapping his hands, except the motion of his hands was up and down, instead of sideways. He stretched, arching his back he looked as if he were reaching for the sky. Maybe he was.

He walked over to the now silent black electric line. He would step close, peek at it, then jump back a few steps. He saw a bird fly through the trees. He walked sneaky-like back over to the big black line, it was just lying there. It was not sputtering or sparking any more. Carl nudged it with his foot, nothing. He leaned over and furtively touched it, yanking his hand back in case it came alive again. It was hot to the touch, but no longer alive. Carl pushed it around a bit with his foot. It did not do anything. It was no longer any fun.

Carl looked around, soaking in his surroundings. Some where in the Woods he could hear a creek bubbling along, he heard leaves rustle, maybe a squirrel, he could hear the song of the bugs. He heard his stomach growl, realized he was hungry it was time to go home. A little boy walking down a gravel road, going home to get something to eat. To see a Mother he loves. He was humming. The first words to the tune he was humming were: "Scooby- Dooby Doo, where are you? I need some one to lean on"…

BRANDON'S SATURDAY

It has been said little girls are made of sugar and spice and everything nice. Little boys on the other hand, have been described being concocted of spiders and snails and puppy dog tails. Perhaps not all little girls fit this description, as cute as it may be, and there are many little boys who are all of this stuff and more; this is a tale of a little boy who is made up of a little bit of all these ingredients, and a few no one has yet to think of. His name is Brandon, and Brandon is everything a parent could want in a little boy, with the exception of being well behaved. This is something Brandon will not be accused of for years to come.

Brandon is a tow headed boy whose hair is not really blonde, but then again not really brown. His hair is so finely spun, it almost never gets tangled, but this could be because it stands straight up on most places of his head. He thinks this is just nifty as can be, and would shy away from a comb quicker than a snake. Wait, he likes snakes, it is combs and baths which terrify him.

This particular sunny Saturday afternoon, Brandon is forced to confront the dreaded comb because his Mom has invited as many of her family over as she could bribe with upside-down pineapple cake and decaffeinated coffee. The guest list includes two sisters, one spinster aunt, an uncomfortable boyfriend (one of the sister's acquisitions) and a nasty tempered miniature poodle named Baby Cakes.

Brandon is in the upstairs bathroom standing on his little stool gazing rather vacantly into the mirror over the sink. Brandon is under strict orders from his Mother to wash his face, brush his teeth, and much to his horror; comb his hair. He started out with the best intentions of achieving everything his Mother ordered, however, just to be safe, he locked himself in the bathroom.

First he grabbed his Mickey Mouse tooth brush, the one he referred to as "the stupid rat mouth torturer". He unscrewed the cap on the tube and began slowly and carefully spreading the paste over the top of the bristles with his left hand.

He smeared enough Colgate Fluoride Enriched Toothpaste on

to the brush to clean a zebra's teeth.   This progressed so smoothly he ran the paste over the bristles, up the handle, in between his thumb and forefinger, and came to a halt at the crook inside his elbow. He surveyed his work for a moment, pleased with the straight line of paste he had made. He also enjoyed the way the paste made the skin on his arm tingle.

Brandon then carefully inserted the brush into his mouth and began to vigorously scrub his teeth…

All of a sudden, Brandon became a Lion Tamer.   The lion has a sore tooth and Brandon has to pull it out.   It was a great giant of a beast and was backed into the corner of a cage.   The whole Clown troop from the Circus came to watch Brave Brandon the Lion Tamer risk life and limb to help the poor lion. What a hero! Everyone loved him!   Brandon heard everyone gasp as he walked into the cage. One little clown lady fainted dead away and hit the ground with a thump. Brandon glanced through the bars of the cage and said "Its OK, this critter just thinks he's mean", and winked at the crowd. He could hear the clowns whispering amongst themselves how there could not be anyone as incredibly courageous as the fearsome Brandon.

Brandon was sticking his hand into the Lion's mouth, a great gaping maw filled with giant sharp teeth and Lion's breath, the beast began to growl. A low mean sound full of menace, when all of the sudden…

" BRANDON!!!!!!! ARE YOU DONE YET??!!
OUR COMPANY WILL BE HERE ANY MINUTE! HURRY UP!!" Brandon's Mother yelled from down stairs.   Brandon looked in the mirror with a grimace, foiled again.

Brandon reached down and twisted the water faucet to the waterfall position, leaned over, rinsed out his mouth, sneezed when he got a nose full of water, giggled, and began to wash the excess tooth paste slobber yuck from his face, hands, and arms.   He looked over at the comb sitting on the counter as if it might bite him, then carefully reached over and picked it up. He slowly began running the comb

94

through his damp hair. He combed his hair to the left, "Nah". He combed it to the right, "Nope". He combed it straight back, "Yep, that'll work". Now he fancied he looked like a fighter pilot just coming back from the war.

He had shot down the dreaded Red Baron. His uniform was tattered and torn but covered with medals... Brandon the Fighter Plane Ace, he had shot down more stinky enemy planes than anybody ever in the history of aviation, he had......

"WHAT...ARE...YOU...DOING IN THERE!!"

Brandon said "Combin my hair Ma, just like you tole me to". She replied "Unlock this door and I mean right now this very minute!" Brandon looked in the mirror and rolled his eyes, then jumped off his stool and walked over to the door, unlocked and opened it. She was standing in the doorway with her hands on her hips. She was wearing a sundress which had a giant red flower pattern all over it. Her hair was pulled back into a severe pony tail which Brandon thought she might ought to loosen up before it stretched her face off. Brandon did not mention this to her, he was brave, but not dumb. His Mom said "Our company will be here any minute and I want everything to be perfect, what in the world have you done to your hair? And look at the mess in the sink. My goodness child, what am I going to do with you?"

She placed both of her hands, one on each of Brandon's shoulders, turned him around, and marched him over to the sink. Brandon hated this. In his mind she was the Evil General and was walking him out to the firing line, any minute he expected her to pull out a blindfold and offer him a cigarette. Our Hero had been captured. Now he was going to pay the ultimate price. Only he knew there was a whole battalion of Green Beret with machine guns and long curved swords just waiting for him to nod his head and begin the rescue operation.

She picked up the comb from the sink counter and began running it through his hair. "You have the prettiest hair. I just do not know why you insist upon making it stand straight up". She could not see him rolling his eyes or his lips moving mimicking every word she said. Although Brandon shortly stopped paying attention to what she was actually saying; her lips were moving and her voice was working, but all Brandon was hearing was Blah, Blah, blah; blabbity blabbity, blabbity; blah, blah, blah.

"Are you listening to me young man? I said to go into your room and put on your clean blue jeans and the nice red pullover your Aunt Jenny got you for Christmas". Brandon sighed deeply and said "Yes Maam", then trudged down the hall towards his room. This was becoming the most dreadful day of his life he thought.

He rummaged through his dresser drawers in search of the clothes his Mother told him to wear. There was a pair of blue jeans. "Nope, got holes" They went sailing across the room, maybe under these shorts, whoosh, whoosh, over his shoulder into the toy box. Where in the heck are they? He turned around frustrated. Oh, there they are, folded up on the bed. Mom must have put them there.

Brandon poked one leg into the jeans, gripped the waist band and pulled it up. While standing he lifted his other leg and was struggling to get it into his pants when he lost his balance, teetered for a moment, and fell to the floor with a thud.

Brandon the Gangster was getting dressed. He was going to a party with a bunch of Movie Stars in Hollywood. His Tommy-gun was on the dresser. All of the sudden a shot rang out and the glass in the window shattered. Brandon hit the floor like a cat. He said "Oh no, it's the G-men, they found me". Bullets began crashing through the walls, the room was being riddled. Feathers were flying everywhere, they murdered a pillow! But Brandon the Gangster had nerves of steel. He crawled over to the bed. He could not get to his Tommy-gun on the dresser, but luckily had stored a box of grenades under his bed. He was going to get those dirty rats! He was going to blow them into next week, he was going to...

"BRANDON! HURRY UP! THEY ARE BEGINNING TO ARRIVE!" His Mom yelled from the kitchen. Drats thought Brandon.

He stood up, put on his shirt, making sure to mess up his hair, and then walked out of his room. He walked over to the stairs and sat down on the top step. He looked down the carpeted steps. He studied the mahogany hand rail which ran up the side of the stairway. He was thinking of interesting ways to dispose of old jello when his Mom yelled up the stairs informing him everyone was here and to come down. Brandon sighed in such a way you would think all of the chocolate in the world had just turned into broccoli.

For a moment Brandon thought of his Aunt Jenny. She loved to pinch the blood out of his cheeks and he hated it, hag. He stood up and was bracing himself to go down the stairs when the light bulb of an idea went pop right over his head. He yelled "OK MOM, I'LL BE RIGHT DOWN". Then he rushed to the bathroom. He climbed up on the stool and opened the medicine cabinet over the sink and there it was. It only took a minute and Brandon was ready to go.

When he got downstairs they were all sitting at the kitchen table. Brandon thought briefly of the Spanish Inquisition. They were all wearing that goofy adult look on their faces which Brandon couldn't stand. They were all so grown-up. Brandon hated them. They could sit for hours drinking coffee and talking, how in the world that could be fun Brandon could not for the life of him understand.

The only one Brandon really liked was Uncle Willy. Uncle Willy always told stories that made Aunt Jenny turn red as a tomato. Brandon thought Uncle Willy was just fine for a grown-up. Uncle Willy was always pouring something from a bottle he kept in his jacket into his coffee, no one would tell Brandon what it was and every time he asked Uncle Willy, his Uncle only said " It's toleration, you'll understand some day", and then he'd wink at Brandon. His Mom only invited Uncle Willy over on Holidays, Brandon did not understand. As a matter of fact, Brandon did not understand grown-ups at all.

Brandon walked slowly to the table. His Mother had a chair pulled out for him right between her and Aunt Jenny, great. Aunt Jenny was wearing a navy blue dress with white polka dots splattered all over it. On her head was perched a white straw hat with a wide brim. The hat had a navy colored band stretched around it with a yellow silk flower poking up out of the side of it. In her lap sat a tiny scraggly poodle with a look of severe distaste on its snout.

Brandon crawled onto the chair and sat down. The first thing to happen was Aunt Jenny exclaimed "Oh what a precious little boy, let me have a look at you", Brandon squirmed and looked at her as if she had a mouthful of spiders. Aunt Jenny reached over with those painted claws she called hands and tried to get a grip on Brandon's cheeks. Her fingers slid right off. She looked a little befuddled and immediately tried again with the same result. Brandon was exercising every muscle in his little body not to start giggling.

Brandon's Mother looked over at him and grabbed his little chin. Her fingers slid right off his face. She gave him her Darth Vader look, and then said to everyone at the table, "Oh, I forgot to mention, but Brandon's little face got some kind of rash and we have to keep VASI-LINE on it". She looked Brandon right square in the eyes and said "Don't we Sugar Pop?"

Brandon knew he was headed for the Dungeon now. He mumbled "Yes Maam". Brandon's Mom was staring him down. "Now Honey, you sit right there with Mommy and your Aunties, oh, and this nice gentleman who is your Aunt Lacy's guest. His name is Henry. Now you be nice and say hello to every one".

Brandon put on his best set of Doe eyes and looked at Aunt Jenny, he said "Hello Aunt Jenny, I love your fat" her eyes widened; Brandon's Mom kicked him under the table and said, "Yes, it is a lovely hat isn't it?" Brandon thought, foiled again. Brandon looked over the table at his Aunt's Beverly and Lacy and said "Hello Aunties", he looked at Henry and said "Pleased to meet you sir, are you friends with the nice man Aunt Lacy brought over here last week?" Aunt Lacy was sipping her cup of coffee and spilt most of it on her dress.

Brandon's Mom looked like she swallowed a bumble bee and said "Oh Honey, you must have him confused with your Uncle Willy". Brandon looked over at his Mom and was about to comment when she gave him her famous I am the Ice Queen look. And he decided silence was the better part of valor. He mumbled quietly "Oh, you're right", all the while feeling like a coward. His Mom said, "Of course I am

98

Honey, now you be still and eat some cake while we all catch up with each other".

Brandon didn't really understand what catching up with each other meant, other than he was now trapped with them until they got done. He sighed and slumped into his chair as if all the oxygen went out of him. Here it was a beautiful Saturday afternoon, and he was stuck with his stupid Mom, and her stupid sisters, especially stupid Aunt Jenny. Then there was Henry. Brandon grinned to himself, now that guys reallllly stupid.

Brandon's eyes glazed over.

Captain Brandon of the Starship Galaxy Invader was sitting in the Control Chair of his space rocket. He looked at the various dials and gauges and decided his speed was just about right. He was traveling at super mega-zap velocity, if all things went well he would arrive at the Martian Colony in record speed. He was adjusting the straps of his seat belt when the giant communicator screen flashed on at the front of the ship. Captain Brandon looked up startled.

On the screen were five giant alligators sitting at a table. They were drinking coffee and nibbling cake. The Leader of the Alligators was wearing a white dress with a red flower pattern. She was speaking to the second in command alligator who was wearing a white straw hat with a stupid looking flower sticking out of it. Captain Brandon figured the flower must indicate some sort of rank. There were three other alligators sitting across from the two Head alligators. They looked particularly evil but were not speaking.

The Head alligator, the one in the white dress was saying it was terribly important they begin taking over the World. The second alligator was nodding her long ugly green nose in agreement. Captain Brandon was watching intently when he noticed the second in command alligator had a lizard in her lap. It was a vicious looking creature, it looked at Brandon and started to growl and hiss, it bared its teeth…

"BRANDON, BRANDON. Sit up and pay attention Brandon.

And stop bothering Aunt Jenny's puppy". Brandon looked over at his mother, his eyes a little foggy and said "Yes Maam". Brandon's Mother started talking, she was saying how awful the economy was and how an honest person could not seem to get by anymore. She just did not know what to do. Aunt Lacy was murmuring agreement. Aunt Lacy said her friend Henry was an accountant and it was criminal what he got paid for it, him with a college education and all. Henry sat there looking as if his foot was in a bucket full of snakes. Aunt Jenny was petting the rat she called a dog and whispering "My little precious, precious puppy" and Aunt Beverly looked as if she were counting jelly beans on the surface of the table.

Brandon was quietly plotting his escape.

Brandon thought about it and decided he was already probably going to get the Chinese water torture after everyone left because of the Vaseline stunt; so what did he have to lose? Brandon made his decision. He had been sitting there quietly for what seemed like weeks. He looked at his Mother, she was talking. He looked at everyone else, they were listening to his Mother. He looked at Aunt Jenny and she was whispering to her dog, the dog was glaring at Brandon.

Brandon made eye contact with Aunt Jenny. She had momentarily stopped whispering to Baby-Cakes. With slow and intent deliberation, Brandon raised his right hand. Never taking his eyes off of Aunt Jenny, he extended his index finger, and gave her an evil smile. She tentatively smiled back at him. It was then Brandon plunged his finger up his nose all the way to his middle knuckle. Aunt Jenny's eyes widened and Brandon started to dig. He was looking for a special nugget. He was a miner…

Brandon the Miner, walking through Gold mines deep under the California earth. He was wearing a metal hat with a lamp attached to it. In one hand he held a cage with a canary, in the other a small pick axe. The lamp was casting a pale stream of light in front of him as he walked through the Mine searching for chunks, nuggets, and big crusty lumps of…

"BRANDON!! WHAT DO YOU THINK YOU ARE DO-ING!! Get your finger out of your nose this instant!" Brandon looked at his Mother, the dog began barking. Aunt Lacy spilled her coffee again. Henry was laughing while Aunt Jenny wrestled with Baby Cakes in her lap. Aunt Beverly still looked as if she were counting jelly beans on the table cloth. Must have forgotten to take her medicine again; and Brandon was pretty sure his plan was a success.

Brandon's Mom looked around the table at everyone and said "Oh for heavens sakes Brandon, why don't you go out and play or something". Brandon looked at his Mother with his second best set of doe eyes, and very solemnly said. "Yes Maam" He excused himself from the table and walked out the back door. The door shut with a tiny phlink…

Brandon the Bank Robber; he was running wildly through the forest, he had just made a daring escape from the horrible prison. No one could keep him in jail. He was the Great BRANDON!!!!!!!!!…

Morton woke up with a start. He had been doing this with great fre-
quency of late. He remembered dreaming of a sun drenched field
where there was tall green grass waving in the wind. Entire sections of
it seemed to lean backwards and forwards, like an ocean of great green
surf pitching towards an unknown shore. The grass was a sea and Mor-
ton was a ship passing through it. He remembered the sun on his face
and shoulders, felt the breeze-tears forming in the corners of his eyes,
he raised his face opening his mouth inhaling blue skies and hills cov-
ered in greenery. He stretched his arms wide, and then spun round and
round, laughing with the sun and the sky; cotton white clouds spread-
ing through and azure blue heaven reaching into a horizon promising
to never end. What a dream! What a dream! The wind in his hair, the
sun on his face, what a dream!

And God did that piss him off. Morton opened his eyes into
the darkness, the deep purple black darkness, the dark. "No" Morton
corrected, it was not just dark. "Oh no", just dark was okay with him,
just dark you could still see shit. But no, this dark he woke up in was
the kind of dark you could only find if you held your breath and stuck
your head up an elephant's ass. That's the kind of dark this was; and
Morton despised it.

Morton tried to stretch, banged both elbows and started mut-
tering profanities that would make a sailor blush. He reached with his
hand to push the surface eight inches in front of his face, a damned
uncomfortable thing to do, he tried to press it again and it would not
give. "What the hell?" he whispered under his breath. "Oh yeah, shit.
I forgot" He reached over and around his chest, fumbled in the space
by his left ear until he his fingers found the little steel ring attached to
one end of a small intricately linked chain.

He placed the index and middle finger of his hand through the
cold metal of the ring, gripped it, and gave it a sharp tug. The chain
gave and the force releasing it caused his arm to shoot across his face.
He felt the chain run under his nose, it felt like the blade of a serrated

saw. He pushed the surface in front of his face straight up and suddenly felt fresh air wash all around him. He sat up. He was really, really, really fucking pissed off.

"Damned frigging son of an Arabian whores after-birth! Fecal remains of a rabid gorilla! Spawn of an inbred ape!" Morton enjoyed using profanity, using profanity made him feel alive for some reason, and in Morton's view, anything making him feel alive was alright by him. You see, Morton is a vampire.

"Damned fucking dreams about sunshine and grass and all sorts of unnecessary horse shit! Can't get out of this coffin because I had to put a safety lock on it to keep the stupid peasants from driving a damn stake through my heart; assholes!" Morton was supremely pissed off.

"Damned if they are still angry about me killing that stupid old lady. Hell, she was almost dead anyway. Lying in her bed barely breathing; I did her a favor. How was I supposed to know she was the Sheriff's grandmother? It's not like they put a sign over her bed saying, HEY! DON'T SUCK GRANDMA'S BLOOD, because if you do, we will sic every superstitious moron with a wooden stake in shed on your ass and hunt you like a dog. Oh no, they couldn't do that could they? Bunch of pricks"

Morton had been trying to be nice (at least as nice as you could expect a vampire to be). He came into town on a fishing boat for Christ's sakes! He thought he would break the town in easy. The first few weeks he only killed vagrants and winos (suffering several hangovers from the latter mind you). Hell, he would have continued to kill the vagrants and winos if there would have been any left.

He could not get over how ungrateful and irritating towns-folk could be. Nobody was bitching when he was exterminating the bums; he never heard a peep from the gendarmes. The only thing he read in the local newspapers was how nicely the community had been shaping up to. No one mentioned the puncture wounds on the bum's necks. The town just rolled them into a community grave and gave them a cheery good riddance.

"Just who in the hell did the town *think* was getting rid of the transients? The City Council? Sons of bitches! Every last one of them"

Morton knew this was bound eventually happen, he would kill one politically incorrect victim and the humans would start a damned revolt.

His buddy Frankenstein only dumped *one* little girl down a well and the humans made a bonfire out of his ass (well, maybe not HIS ass per se, but it was someone's ass damnit!) Hell, the little girl didn't even drown. She was crippled, but you know hey, these things happen. Humans are assholes.

Morton did not know what he was going to do now. Every asshole in town was walking around at night holding hands and carrying torches. This very morning before he went to sleep he had to dig a bullet out of his ass, a silver one no less. And that's how the Gypsy's sold his buddy Wolfy down the river, and Wolfy was bringing them fresh meat for crying out loud! Bunch of dickheads!

He was sitting up in the coffin now, trying to get his nose to sit straight on his face. Damn near cut it off with that stupid chain. Good thing vampires heal quickly, except for a wooden stake through the heart. Shit. That little thought darkened his mood a couple of extra degrees. He had one hand on his nose wriggling it back into place, from a distance it sounded as if he were spitting. If you were to get closer (which I would not if I were you), you could hear it was not spitting in the traditional sense, he was spitting a word; *Pricks…prickssss…pricksss,* only Morton could hiss when he was cursing.

After he stopped fiddling with his nose he started doing some serious thinking. Theoretically he could go another day or two without turning someone into a quivering slurpee. But damnit! He did not want to. "Why can't they understand I have special dietary needs to consider? It's not like I can just walk stroll down to the nearest café and order a cheese burger with some fries" For one wistful moment he remembered a time he could, and then snapped out of it. "Damnit!" Don't get distracted now he chided himself. "You have to figure something out now and you have to do it damn quick."

Morton allowed himself a small fantasy. He imagined himself walking into a restaurant, some cute little waitress would sashay over to his table "May I take your order Sir?" He would look squarely into her eyes and say "No thank you sweet heart, I would rather wrap my lips around your neck and give you a hickey you will never forget. I would like to sink my fangs into your jugular and feel your red hot frothy blood shoot down my throat like shit squirting out of a ducks ass" he leaned back and chuckled at the little daydream. "Beats the hell out of that sun crap" he muttered to himself.

His stomach growled. Now what to do about the assholes in this town he pondered. He was scratching his chin with one hand while the other one was poking at the hole in his butt cheek the silver bullet left. He was deep in thought when he heard a rattle at the front door of the mausoleum he was hiding in. "Oh great" he thought "Speak of the assholes and they shall appear. Now what am I going to do?" He did not think they would check this place for several days, but he thought, "got to give them credit, they are smart assholes".

He was about to lock himself back into the coffin and take his chances when the big marble door in the front creaked open. He was expecting to see a shit-load of assholes with really bad attitudes storm in, but there standing in the doorway, silhouetted by moonlight, stood a little boy.

Morton rose as quickly from his resting place as any supernatural being you could imagine. In a flash he was standing by the child peeking out the open door behind him. There was nothing but moonlit darkness. Long shadows cast by the tombstones backlit by a harvest moon. There was a weeping willow with branches reaching in a circle as if trying to grasp the ground and hold the grave-stones; creepy shit like that, but no more humans. Morton thought "What now?" He looked at the little boy. The boy looked back. "Anybody with you?" Morton said. The little boy replied "Nope"

"You're sure?"

"Yep"

"Nobody with torches, carrying hammers and sticks? Garlic wrapped around their necks looking scared and pissed off?"

The little boy thought for a second and then said "Nah, I would have noticed sumpthin like that" Morton blew out his breath "Whew! Good thing, that could have really screwed up my day" or night, he thought to himself.

The little boy stood staring at him. Morton said "What the hell are you looking at kid?" The boy replied "I'm looking at you Mister. Are you that vampire everybody's talking about?" Morton straightened up a little, cleared his throat and said "Yeah, now you mention it, I am. What do you think about that you little urchin?"

The little boy squinched up his face, looked Morton up and down, and said "You don't look like no vampire to me" Morton was deeply offended. "What the hell do you mean I don't look like no vampire to you?!" he whined. "Just how many vampires have you ever seen you little rat?"

The boy looked at his fingers as if he were going to count them, he then reached up to scratch his head and said "I've seen bunches. I got me a book from the library called Unicorns, Witches and Vampires. I looked at all the pictures of vampires and I never saw one that looked like you"

Morton snorted (it was an ugly sound since his nose was not quite solid yet). "Now look here you little snip. I am a vampire. And if I wanted to, I could bite your scrawny neck and drink every drop of blood out of your little bony body. The only problem is, there is probably not enough there to go to all the trouble. What do you think of that you little fart?"

"I think you're lying"

"Lying! Why you little!...what do you mean I'm lying?! You look at one bloody book about vampires and now you are an expert! I ought to, I ought to…well, I ought to something you little dung heap!"

Morton was fuming. He could not believe the cheek of this little tramp, he was thinking of the most painful place to bite the little shit when the boy said "What's your name Mister Vampire?"

"Huh? What? Oh, my names Morton. What's it matter to you?"

The boy grinned "That don't sound like no vampire name to me"

Morton sneered "That don't sound like no vampire name to me" he mimicked.

This was exasperating, here he was expecting to be raided by five hundred or so asshole towns people, every last one of them wanting to pin him to the ground like a nocturnal butterfly; but instead, he was arguing his identity with a little kid who had to be the youngest smartass in the history of vampire-dom.

I'll bet Count Dracula never had to put up with this shit thought Morton. Drac lived in a town where the people were so shit scared of him they would send him a virgin once a week. It must have been the castle, people respect castles. Morton was where he could get a castle, maybe Drac had a real estate agent with some suggestions "Oh hell, I couldn't afford it anyway" he thought.

No, Morton was stuck in this dumpy little town out in the middle of fucking nowhere listening to some kid who would probably ask him to play marbles any second now.

"No I won't"

Morton about jumped out of his skin. He looked at the kid and said "What did you say?"

"Nothin"

"Oh yes you did you little brat. I distinctly heard you say something. Now what was it before I bite your ass, and I promise it will not be a pleasant sensation"

The little boy squinted his eyes, gave the vampire a quizzical look and said "I think you are imagin'in things Mister. Are you sure you're feeling okay?"

"FEELING OKAY?! Well of course I'm feeling okay. What's not to feel okay about? I got a town full of assholes looking under every rock hoping to find me and ram a sharpened hunk of dead tree through my unsuspecting sleeping ass; but here I am dealing with the world's shortest smart aleck instead of hauling my supernatural ass out to the next village. Yes!! I am feeling okay!! I don't have one stinking problem in the whole stinking world! Any other questions Tiny Tim?"

The little boy sucked his lips into his mouth, he was in deep thought. He shuffled his feet back and forth kicking imaginary gravel. He looked up at Morton and said "You still could Mister"

Morton was pacing around lost in his own world, he looked up at the sound of the boy's voice, a confused look on his face. He had not been paying attention. "Huh? What's that boy? I could still do what?"

"You could still go to the next village"

Morton looked at the boy "Oh yeah right. I am gong to take the advise of the first munchkin who happens to wander into my hide out. Yeah, thanks but no thanks. Now shut up you little shit, can't you see I'm thinking". "Little Prick" Morton exclaimed under his breath "Humans, who needs em?" Except for dinner that is, Morton smiled.

He was pacing again. He did not need this sort of trouble. It was difficult enough to be a respectable vampire in this day and age, now he was a baby sitter. This was disgusting he surmised. From behind his back he heard the boy "Don't say I didn't warn you"

Morton thought, what the hell is that supposed to mean? And then it dawned on him. What in the hell is a little boy doing wandering around a graveyard in the middle of the night? Especially in this town…the town's people have their children under lock and key because of him.

Morton was in the act of spinning around when he felt the fist punch on his back. He looked down to see the sharpened end of the stake slide out of the left side of his chest. To his horror blood spurted out in front of him. Looking down he could distinguish his blood on the splinters of the wooden point. He could ascertain the wood grain. Morton knew he had been suckered. The last two words to escape his mouth were "Oh shit" He dropped to his knees, the weakness consuming him. He would no longer be worrying about the town-people. He realized he had been royally fucked.

The little boy walked around Morton to face him. Morton was blinking rapidly. He had both his fists wrapped around the stake protruding from his chest. The boy looked at him without humor or mercy and said "I came here to warn you. It did not have to come to this. But oh no, you had to be Mister potty-mouthed vampire. I heard everything you were thinking, don't think I didn't. You are a disgrace to vampires everywhere. You are getting everything you deserve trouble maker"

Morton was looking at this child vampire, he fell backwards and was now splayed over bent legs. He tried to talk but only a crimson froth washed over his lips. The boy was standing over him, eyes glowing bluish red now, evil incarnate. "Look here Morton, it was enough you were a slime-bag of a vampire to begin with, but that was not why

I killed you" Morton was fading fast, he felt somewhere in his soul it was a relief. The boy was glaring at him, his eyes no longer glowing; the last thing Morton's previously immortal ears heard was the boy saying:

"I killed you because…THIS IS MY TOWN"

My Father was a mysterious man. I know people say this all the time in reference to their Pater, however, in mine and my brothers case, even the extended family as a whole; my Father was a mysterious man.

For instance, we as a family always drove vehicles not released to the general public years before the general public knew what they were. We were the first family in North Carolina as far as anyone knew, to own an SUV. And if this were not enough, there was a phone in the vehicle, when no one had ever considered this as a possibility, much less a necessity. We probably would have been more popular had people not been just a little frightened of this, which was in their opinion, impossible technology.

In my Father's study, he had a functioning computer with access to internet facilities many years before the internet became a household word. He would spend hours at his computer and if my brother or I asked what he was doing, he would just shrug and say "Oh, tinkering around". Now I am able to look back with the retrospect of a man, this must have been *some* tinkering.

My Father is a big and burley man. If he shaved in the morning, by mid afternoon he was beginning to resemble a bear. He has deep brown eyes which reflect gold in the right light, and possesses a voice which is gentle as the wind blowing through an oak tree, or as booming as drum and cymbals. Women always looked at him with questioning desire in their eyes and wonton posture on their bodies. Dad never once seemed to notice the attention women so freely tried to give him; he had his lady, and that was my Mom. He opened doors for her, and pulled out her chair at the dinner table, even when we were at home. He still does.

The only time my Father gave me a beating was when I was eleven years old and told my Mother she needed to mind her own business. He sat me straight right away. I could talk to him however I wanted to; if I dared, but I would respect my Mother. She was his woman a long time before she was my Mother, and no one would treat her with disrespect, including me, he explained this to me in a way I would never forget. I only hope when I have a wife, I can love her in this way.

But my Fathers relationship with Mother is not what this story is about. This story is about how a mysterious man set out to make his sons men. I know there are many stories of how fathers treat sons, and some are good, some bad, some not to be mentioned; this is just our story, and this was the turning point of my life. I knew at the time something special was happening, but there was no way for me to know this would be the end all be all of everything I would hope to become, this would be the ground where my father planted the seed of my manhood.

My name is Grant. My brother's Robert. In the spring of 1987 is the two weeks all this took place. I was fourteen years old, my brother three years older. My brother is close to being the smartest person as I have ever known. He has never had a grade under an A. He has never played a sport he did not excel in, he has never breathed a breath in a day he was not sure he had control of, in short, he is probably a genius. His only downfall is hubris, he does not just dislike authority and all its guises; he hates it.

Sometimes my father says Robert has been in trouble since the day he was born. But trouble does not last for the genius. He will prevail when all fail around him. Failure dares not to visit Robert, he will not allow it. When I was in the fourth grade there was a kid who decided to fight me. I had to this point in my life been a gentle soul, and still am to some degree. I came home with a mashed and bloody nose, skint knees, and all of the things which go with a youthful fight. My brother took one look at me and said "Who?"

I said it didn't matter. Robert corrected me. He told me I had to have my own honor, he said outcomes did not matter, outcomes are natural, but he looked at me and knew I had been scared by this boy, and he looked me in the eye and told me tomorrow I would learn of honor. The next day he found this other boy and took us out behind the bleachers at the school. There was no one there but the three of us.

I did not know what was going to happen, and the boy who had hurt me thought Robert was going to hurt him. Robert surprised us both. He very calmly looked at me and said "He hurt you yesterday and scared you, are you scared now?" and I was. But I said no. He grinned. He looked at the boy and said "You kicked Grant's ass yesterday, but that was yesterday, do it today" The boy looked at Robert who was older than us and said "Why, you just going to kick my ass if I do".

Robert laughed. I will never forget his laugh this day. He looked at the kid and said "Nope, you got me all wrong. I am not going to lift a finger. You hurt him and I will let you. I just will not allow him to be scared of you" The kid looked at Robert like he was crazy, so did I. Robert looked in my eyes and said one word: "Honor".

I would like to say I returned the favor to the boy by winning a fight. But I can't. Oh, we fought, we fought like cats and dogs, but in the end, he was a tough kid and I was bested. Or at least I thought I was. Turns out, if anything it was a draw. I felt like I had been in a car wreck. In the end, Robert made us shake hands. The boy went one way, my brother and I another. My eye was black, my knuckles scraped, I was limping. But I was not crying. Robert looked at me after we had walked for awhile. He said "You scared anymore?" I thought about it, I knew I was hurting, I knew I was bleeding in a few places, but I thought about it and looked at my brother and said "No, not anymore". He looked at me and smiled; he said "Now you know honor". I have never been scared of any one after that day. And that is who my brother is.

So in the spring of 1987, my Father announced we were going on an adventure. Just him, my brother, and me. He said the men of the family were going on a mans trip, to pack light, and be ready for fun. My brother and I had no idea what was in store, for when Dad said we were doing something, this was the way it was; so we packed like he told us, and on one sunny spring day, a Tuesday if I remember, we loaded up the Cherokee, and off we went.

Dad didn't say much as we backed out of the driveway. He was holding a cup of coffee in one hand and the steering wheel in the other. When we accelerated down the road my brother Robert asked where we were going, Dad smiled and said "South". True to his word we got to the interstate and south was the direction he chose. All the time he was smiling. I think on some level my father knew this was more than just a trip.

We left North Carolina with the radio humming soft country music, the sun was shining and the sky was a blue ocean with fluffy white islands of clouds reaching towards one another. The windows down you could hear the tires caressing the highway; you could hear the crickets and katydids singing from the trees lining the shoulders. The thunder of eighteen wheelers passing us and feel the truck we were in lean in the wind left by these giants. We were three on a journey, a father and his two sons. The purity of our togetherness an echo of fathers and sons walking together from the beginning of time, the only difference was the truck, it could have been a ship, or a wagon, or on horseback, we were the fathers and the sons of humanity. And we were together.

We stopped at tiny roadside cafes for lunch and dinner. Robert and I talked of school; Dad told us stories of when he was in school and when he was a boy. He told us stories about his father, our grandfather. He told us stories of a great-great grandfather who lived on a mountain and wrote a book long before anyone in West Virginia considered reading and writing important. We did not even know we had people in West Virginia. We talked and talked and the roads and the cafes changed, South Carolina became dust behind us as Georgia loomed before us. When we stopped for gas and snacks or lunch or dinner, we could hear the voices of people's accents change. In South Carolina folks had a twang in their speech close to us and those of home. By the time we got to Savanna Georgia, the accents had deepened to a point we had to concentrate to listen to what they were saying.

Dad told us this was a lesson. All people were flesh and bone, but they all had their homes. Where you are from means a great deal about who you are, and who you become, he said. He told us to never make fun of how people talk, because we don't know where they come from or what sort of education they may have enjoyed. He told us because someone sounds different or even stupid, don't mean they are; he said there are folks out there who have never cracked a page in a book and are smarter than the Harvard educated. He said education is important, but it is not everything. He told us how Samuel Clemens, otherwise known as Mark Twain, said to never let schooling interfere with your education. He was in his own way, explaining life.

We passed through Georgia where the trees had changed from towering oaks and pines to weeping willows covered with kudzoo. This was spring, so green was sprouting everywhere you looked, and in the air the scent and fragrance of flowers and new life filled your nostrils and head with a sense of wonder and enchantment. Such is spring in the South. We then drove into Florida.

Nothing much changed initially, when we stopped at a motel or diner, the people's accents became a bit clearer. And as we continued the trek south the trees at first seemed greener, thicker, primordial. We traveled over bridges spanning swamps, scary looking places with strange birds and sounds. Occasionally we would see an alligator sunning itself on a bank. Dad told us to take a long look and remember what we saw, because this was the last of the dinosaurs, but to consider someday when man has failed, they will come again to reclaim their kingdom.

We finally arrived in Key West. The Southern most point of Florida. We drove over a bridge so long my brother and I thought we would be on a bridge forever. And then we were there. Key West was definitely one of the most festive places we had ever been to or imagined. The people were colorful and the weather was hot. We went to our hotel and walking from the truck to the doors, my brother and I thought we were going to melt. We checked in at the front desk and then trudged to our room. Once there, Dad ordered a huge dinner of steaks and fried potatoes. While we ate, Dad spent time talking on the phone. After dinner, he said, let's take a walk.

We walked together through the streets of Key West. There were bars and restaurants, and heat, my God we were sweating. We walked around a corner and there was a guy playing his guitar, the case he carried it in open on the ground, full of quarters and wrinkled dollar bills. Just to his left leaning against a bench was another guitar. My Father looked at the man for a moment, and then asked if he could play the other guitar.

The man sitting said sure, if you want to pick it up. My Dad picked up this old guitar, he ran his fingers over the strings, he tuned the tuning keys; he was very concentrated. Then all of the sudden like kindling being lit by a spark and starting a fire he started to play.

Robert and I looked at each other for a moment, and Dad and this stranger began to play those guitars. They sang together, they played together, this stranger and our Father; and as the instruments worked together a crowd gathered. These men strumming and caressing their instruments on a street in Key West , and us teenaged boys watching with wonder. Dad gave as good as he took. And when they finished, strangers applauded and tossed money into the guitar case. If our Father was not already something amazing in our eyes, he was now a Rock and Roll Star.

Dad stood up smiling and leaned the guitar he was playing on the same bench he picked it off of, pulled a twenty dollar bill from his wallet, and laid it into the guitar case laying on the ground, the stranger protested; Dad said "Thank you for your hospitality, I enjoyed my stay in your home"

Robert and I walked away from that street corner this night in Dad's company, the three of us seemed to glow with our togetherness; I have never felt so connected with anything in my whole life; on a street in Key West, in the spring, two sons and a father. I think I will always feel as if the heat of South Florida was what melted us together, in the spring of 1987.

The next morning we found ourselves on a Sailboat. This was some kind of Sailboat. There was a kitchen, cots to sleep on, a deck to walk on, and Dad said we were going sailing. We untied from the dock before eight am. Robert and I had no idea Dad knew what a sailboat was, much less how to sail into open water like a Viking. But he did, and there we were, sails filled with wind, Dad yelling things like watch out for the boom, come about, drop sails, hoist sails, raise the jib, steady with the mainsheet. So many things I would forget near immediately.

We were out for six days. The days filled with sailing, with watching dolphins and sharks and all sorts of interesting fish swimming by, or leaping out of the water in the distance. Between the ocean and the sky,

I never knew there was so much blue in the world. At night Dad would cook on a small hibachi grill on the forward deck, being insanely careful of the coals. The conversations the three of us participated in on these days and evenings were not of two boys and a man, or even two sons and a father, they were the stuff of men grown, and men growing. Sometimes late at night when immersed in my own recollections and disabused notions; I can still hear my brother and fathers voices blending with the gentle sound of waves lapping against the sides of our vessel. I can feel the boat rocking like a sea born cradle. If I try I can still taste the salty wind on my lips, feel the warm brush of an ocean breeze against my forehead. In my adult life I find myself spending a great deal of pleasant time, still in the spring of 1987.

Four days into our journey, we were sailing in what seemed to be a magnificent day. The sun was bright and hot, the ocean clear and green around us, deep and blue in the distance. God was in his heavens and all was right in the world. When very suddenly the main sail swelled as if by magic and we felt as if the boat was shot out of a catapult. My brother and I were thrilled. When we heard Dad say "Oh shit!" Robert and I were stunned, he never cursed. He then screamed for us to immediately put on our life jackets and the strength in his voice broached no room for discussion. We did as we were told, and watched our beautiful day turn into a waking night mare.

We had ran full into a white squall. A white squall is a wind storm on the oceans surface which seems to appear from nowhere. There are no dark clouds to warn you, no sudden rain or drop in temperature, it is immediate. One minute you are clear sailing, the next you are in a mini cyclone. It is terrifying. Dad was barking orders to drop sail while untying lines and retying others, we did the best we could and dad was fighting the rudder like a mad man. The look on his face was somewhere between concern and joy, from my vantage point of hanging on for dear life with my brother, I actually detected a small strange smile on my fathers lips. Because of my fathers face at this moment, I once again found myself not afraid: My Father and Brother; champions of my soul.

We were tossed around like a toy in a bathtub by an unruly child,

116

I will never know how long this went on, but it seemed like forever. Wind blowing gusts of salty warm seawater burning our eyes and making for slippery hands as we held on to anything solid. At one point the boat near capsized, was literally lying on its side in the turbulent water. The three of us elevated and hanging on to the side furthest from the ocean. The wind was still howling, but seemingly not as loud. We were in the middle of nowhere in the ocean, in a storm, hanging on to a near capsized sailboat like three half drowned monkeys.

My Father yelled over the wind. "BOYS, YOU CAN MAKE YOUR OWN DECISIONS ABOUT GOD AND RELIGION. I WILL NOT TRY TO INFLUENCE YOU. BUT THERE COMES TIMES IN YOUR LIFE LIKE NOW, WHEN YOU HAVE DONE EVERYTHING A MAN CAN DO TO SAVE HIMSELF AND THE ONES HE LOVES, THERES NOT ONE OTHER THING HE CAN ATTEMPT, AND ALL HE HAS LEFT IS FAITH. BELIEVE WHAT YOU WANT, BUT ALWAYS HARBOR AND PROTECT YOUR FAITH, BECAUSE ONE DAY, IT WILL BE ALL YOU HAVE LEFT!" I think we all looked at each other as if it might be the last time we had the opportunity. I saw more clearly this day than I have ever seen in my life. And then, like some kind of magic trick; the wind stopped. I mean stopped. Nothing but clear skies and open water.

With an effort straining muscles that would hurt for two weeks afterwards, we managed to upright the boat. It was a mess. Ropes everywhere, sails a nasty tangle. Anything not tied down missing, but we were alive and laughing, we weathered a White Squall. Dad, Robert, and me, we were ebullient. We were so happy we did not notice the small craft approaching from the distance.

Suddenly we heard a man's voice over a mega-phone. He was yelling in Spanish. The small boat was coming very close, all I remember was it looked like a beat up little motor boat, except for the very clean and glistening machine gun mounted on the forward deck. As the motor boat drew up next to us I could see large men with mustaches and big bellies, their torso's wrapped with belts filled with bullets, and each of them with holstered pistols and evil looking rifles in their hands. Now I got scared.

My Father addressed them in Spanish. Robert and I had no idea what they were saying, but the situation seemed to turn from tense to relaxed. Within minutes these strange men and my father were talking and laughing as if they had been friends their entire lives. Robert and I once again looked at each other exchanging glances filled with wonder because of our father. Turns out the storm had blown us into Cuban waters, and these were representatives of their coast guard coming to question us. They boarded us to have a talk with dad. Within a half hour they gave dad directions back to Florida, helped unfurl the tangled sails, helped to make our little boat ship shape. When they left, they carried two boxes of Twinkies in their hands dad had salvaged from the galley. When the wind caught our sails, I looked back at the Cuban Coast Guards, their little boat, its big machine gun, and these very serious looking men wearing weapons, and they were holding up little yellow sponge cakes and yelling "TWINKIES!"

When we were driving North through Georgia, the trip nearing its end, we were all pretty quiet. The temperature dropped little by little as we traveled north. The sun was still bright in an azure spring sky for as far as you could see. I watched the trees pass us by on either side of the highway. I remember Robert was asleep in the back seat. I was listening to the thrum of the tires against the pavement, listening to the low hum of country music coming out of the radio. I happened to glance at my Father, he was looking at me. He held out his hand, I grasped it, and he shook it as if I were a man. He winked at me and said "You did good out there son, I am proud of you". Then he placed his hand back on the steering wheel and didn't say much of anything else until we got home. My Father was a mysterious man…

For Grant.

"It's not THAT quiet," Billy thought to himself. There was the whir of the refrigerator, his stereo humming because the CD finished. A steady drip, drip, drip, coming from somewhere, the sink or the shower he guessed. "No" he reassured himself, it is not silent…it is still. There is a difference.

He sat in the stillness thinking about the night. A thick headed confusion due to coming down from the booze and drugs made his head feel like a block of wood (one filled with nails sticking into his brain). He could remember his favorite music playing, loud and filled with base and screams. Other people thought of it as "hate music", but fuck them; what did they know about thrash? It was in this music he found his calm, where he discovered his center and found his peace while hurtling through an otherwise difficult world. He found his hate in hating the people who hated his music because they thought it was hateful. What did they know of his life? Hate music? To hell with them he thought to himself.

He tried to clear his head by reaching for a cigarette, and in the dim light of the living room he noticed a stain on his hand. Briefly he tried to focus on that hand while reaching from the couch to grab his pack of smokes with the other. He grabbed the packet and felt, more than noticed the tackiness on his finger-tips as they pressed upon the cellophane of the box. He shook one out, placed it into his lips. His hand was trembling when he fired the lighter, eyes closed as to not see his fingers.

"What the fuck happened last night?" He inhaled the acrid smoke into his lungs, blew it out coughing, realizing he had smoked too many cigarettes the evening before, feeling the pain. He recalled meeting Sheila at the club. She was coked out and being an unreasonable bitch. She wanted him to drop a tab with her and wouldn't take no for an answer. The band was rocking the fuck out and loud as hell and in all the thrash and blast of music and sweat Billy said "What the fuck, why not?" and did.

Three Heinekens later he felt like he was floating inside a helium balloon that was exploding. It felt fan-fucking-tastic! Friday night in the life-style, rock and Goth, fingernails painted black, leather and lace complimented by collars attached to leashes. The music loud, angry and consuming, a place you could scream to the heavens to send you to hell and laugh all the way there.

Billy was high, hyped and more than a little sideways when he and Sheila staggered out into the night. He threw his green beer bottle into the side of a building and the acid coursing through his veins made it tumble gracefully end over end until it shattered into particles of light in his eyes against the red brick wall. They were laughing and stumbling when they got to their neighborhood. The drugs were mad good this night.

Billy finally opened his eyes. He needed a place to put out his cigarette. He brought the filter to his lips for one last drag, his finger-tips brushed his lips, when he licked them he tasted copper and salt. "I would rather stick my head into a guillotine slot than open my eyes right now" he said softly into the morning. He leaned from the couch, found the ashtray by touch, and ground out the cigarette while never opening his eyes.

When they got home, all he wanted was a beer, a blowjob, and maybe some of the kind of sex would make him want to shower for a week while laughing at the moral majority. God he loved Sheila, and not just because they shared the opinion sodomy was the perfect form of birth control, they had an addiction, to each other. She was the freak he wanted more than he understood what true want was, she was his girl, his property; his addict who he had become addicted to; Sheila.

He shook his head "Coming down from this shit is a bitch!" he said to the room. The fog in his head began disperse, the ice-pick of hangover slowly pulling out from his temple. All the colors coalesc-ing in his head began to take shape and form, memory gaining ground slowly to recall the evening. He began to remember: "I'm not getting off of this couch", his voice was hoarse when he said it. "No, no, fuck that! Oh man, this is some shit, some shit!" He closed his eyes so tightly he could feel droplets of tears popping out around the edges of his eyelids, he could feel his long hair laying against his neck and draping over his shoulders, and he could feel the stillness. "It is not silent" he whispered to himself "It is still".

He finally looked at his hands. There was a crust of sorts on his silver rings, he could feel his fingers sticking together, and then remembered the knife. It was this big wooden handled butcher knife he stole it from his father when he left home. "Fuck! Why did I take that fucking knife! Fuck! Fuck! Fuck!" He stood up from the couch shaky and unsteady. "This is a bad dream" he said to himself. "Yeah, that's it, a bad dream. The baddest motherfucker of bad dreams ever; yeah, that's it" he said to himself, ignoring the stains on his hands, shirt and running down his jeans.

In a dream state he walked from the living room to the kitchen. It was all coming back. "Who the fuck wants to eat after a coke and acid binge?" the thoughts were now racing through his no longer high consciousness as he turned the corner into the kitchen. The floor was yellow checkered linoleum, mostly. And there she was. He said "Hi Sheila".

Silence.

She was wearing the leather vest he bought her for her birthday (a good day). He noticed her fishnet stockings were perfect, one leg stretched straight on the floor, the other bent at her knee. As if she were doing a curtsy, or maybe attempting to make a snow angel on the linoleum. Her left arm was stretched out to her side, one wing of an angel, nail polish shiny red. Her right arm curved with her hand holding her cheek as if she were asleep. Her right hand and splayed brunette hair soaking in a pool of blood. "Holy shit" he said out loud. "That's a lot of fucking blood".

Stillness

Billy was standing in the shower. He had brought a beer in with him. After rinsing the shampoo from his hair he reached for the bottle on the ledge of the tub and drank half of it. There was still a brown tinge in the water spiraling down the drain at his feet. He turned his face into the spray of hot water forcing his self to think of anything but last night. The water started losing its temperature. He reached down to turn the knob counterclockwise stopping the spray. He was pleased to notice he saw nothing going down the drain now but soapy swirls. He stood dripping by the commode and finished the beer.

Walking into bedroom he reached for a pack of cigarettes he knew was on the nightstand. He sat down on the edge of the bed and lit a smoke. The digital clock on the dresser read 5:45. The numbers were red he saw as he blew smoke into the room. Funny how he had never noticed the color before, red skies at night he thought. It was Saturday morning. He walked back into the living room ensuring the front door was locked. And then walked back and went to bed.

His head was pounding when he woke up. Daylight streamed through the curtains like boiling acid. He looked at the empty pillow next to him and said "Oh yeah" to no one in the room.

The kitchen smelled of copper, as if someone had filled the sink with pennies and soaked them with hot water. He gazed down at Sheila and said "Sweet-heart, blue is definitely not your color. Seriously, I mean it". He stepped over her outstretched leg avoiding the pool of blood which had spread from her right breast, then opened the refrigerator and grabbed a coke. He closed the door and walked into the living room to turn on the television, it was Saturday afternoon.

Billy was watching a Daffy Duck cartoon when the phone rang. He looked at the receiver, briefly considering answering it, but decided due to the present situation he would let the answering machine catch it. After ringing six times Sheila's recorded greeting filled the room "We were here and you were not, now you are here and we are not, leave a message or don't"-- beep. "Hey Sheila, are you home?" "Billy?"... "Alright guys, this is Liz. When you get this message give a call. There is going to be a band over at Dead Cellar tonight guaranteed to kill us all. I hear they are like Manson but darker. Ta, ta.". The machine beeped again. Billy lit another cigarette.

He was standing over Sheila, thinking. It was late Saturday night, he thought he should probably do something, he just didn't know what. Her hair was flat and matted on the floor in dried blood. He thought "I guess I should wash that, she hates it when her hair gets greasy". He reached down and gently grasped her under her armpits, pliable. He did not know rigor mortis had come and gone. He lifted slowly attempting to maneuver her into a sitting position while peeling her hair out of the dried pool of blood.. "Goddamn that shits sticky" he said to her.

He was extricating her hair from the blood, her head lolling when her bowels released. The smell was stifling. Billy said "Damn Sheila; what'd you eat yesterday?" and laughed. He carried her to the bathroom like a groom would carry his new bride over the matrimonial threshold. Once there he placed her in the tub as gently as possible. He removed her vest. She was wearing nothing under it. He slipped the skirt from around her waist and pulled her thong off, then carefully rolled the fishnets down her thighs, over her calves to pull them off from her feet. The only unpleasant part of her to look at he thought was the huge gash across her throat. He walked into the bedroom, rifled through one of the drawers in dresser, found a silver scarf and went back to the bathroom.

He tied the scarf around her neck, stepped back to inspect his handiwork and decided now she was a beautiful as she had ever been. He turned the knob clockwise to start the bathwater and watched as it slowly filled the tub around her, he checked it often to make sure it was not too hot.

Billy took his time. He washed and conditioned her hair. He scrubbed the inside of her knees with the loofah, just the way he knew she liked it. He emptied and refilled the tub until there was no more red water to bother with. He carried her from the bathroom and laid her on the bed where he dried her from head to toe with one of her favorite big poofy pink towels. He brushed out her long brunette hair, being careful to get the tangles. And then put her in the concert t-shirt she like to sleep with. He tucked her into bed. He was sitting on the edge of the bed when he said "Do you feel better hun?"

Silence

"Hey, I'm sorry about last night, I'm not sure what happened. We were arguing; and HIGH as hell" he laughed. "You were trying to cook something, I don't know, some kind of fucking stir fry or something. Come on babe, who the fuck cooks stir fry on acid? What the fuck were you thinking?"

Stillness

He laughed again and then sighed, "Then you started in on me, you know?"

Silence

"Babe, why can't we talk unless we are high and fighting?" He looked at her.

Stillness

He opened the nightstand drawer, pulled out a small tray and began rolling a joint. "You know" he said as he was manipulating the rolling papers between his fingers, "How the fuck are we gonna explain this to our friends? Did you fucking think of that before you pissed me off? Hell no you didn't! That's the problem with you Sheila, you never think ahead". He licked the paper from end to end to seal the joint. "That's always been your problem…never thinking ahead". He looked at her.

Silence

Billy picked up the blue Bic lighter laying by the bed lamp. He carefully lit the joint so as to get an even burn. He inhaled deeply, laid his head back onto the pillow on his side of the bed. He watched as he exhaled the smoke, seeing the reflection of it and him, and her, in the dresser mirror. He looked over at Sheila. She was just as beautiful as he had ever seen her. He pressed the joint to his lips and inhaled too deeply and spasmed into a coughing fit. He coughed until he saw red dots in front of his eyes. He looked at Sheila and said "You want some of this babe?"

Stillness

"Guess not" he said. The weed started to work on him. He felt the billowing mellow reaching over and through him, gently bumping through the insides of his skull. His skin started feeling warm, a little overheated, and when he closed his eyes it was the slow motion of light escaping from his head, and not the light receding, he WAS light. This was some primo weed. "God we used to have fun doing this babe" he heard himself say. "Didn't we?"

Silence

"You're kind of quiet tonight Sheila"

Stillness

"Are you still mad at me?"

Silence

He rolled over on one elbow and looked at her closed eyes. "I know what you need babe"

Stillness

"So you want to play it like that?" he said. The room was in and out of focus for him, "Shit, this is some seriously good weed" he mentioned to no one. "Sheila, you know how much I love you don't you?"

Silence

He shifted towards her and worked his hand up under her shirt and began kneading her breast. "You are cold babe" he said and grinned. "But damn, those nips are horny hard". He pulled her shirt up, careful not to disturb the scarf around her neck. He began licking and nibbling the nipple on her left breast, then moved to her right. His hand moved down to her shaved vagina, he whispered in her ear "God, we are good together babe. Don't ever leave me" He pushed his middle finger into her, and then his index. "Sheila, this going to be soooo good; I don't think you have ever been this tight". Billy rolled on top of Sheila and made love to her.

Stillness

Billy walked out of the kitchen with a Heineken in his hand. In the darkened bedroom he sat down on the bed next to Sheila. He fished a roach out of the ashtray and took a swig of the beer. He lit the roach inhaling deeply and looked at the ceiling tiles.

Silence

Stillness

Silence

Stillness

Silence

Stillness.

Inhale…exhale…drink.

Billy looked at the clock, 5:45. LCD glowing red, how appropriate he thought, and a Sunday no less. He reached over with his left hand and stroked Sheila's forehead and said "You know I love you babe, but you're starting to smell kind of funny".

Silence

"Man, you don't talk as much as you used to. To tell you the truth, you seem sorta stiff anymore" he laughed.

Stillness

Billy reached into the top drawer of the nightstand, "Gonna get high again babe"

Silence

He rolled over on top of her and perched on his left elbow. With the fingers on his right hand he lightly pulled her eyelids open. It was too dark for him to see the blue milkshake of death they had turned into. He looked into darkness, pressed his lips to hers sticking his tongue into her cold mouth. He pressed the barrel of the revolver to his temple and said "I love--------". The rest was lost to explosion.

Stillness

Silence

Stillness

Silence

The phone began ringing. Six rings later Sheila's taped voice said into the stillness "We were here and you were not, now you are here and we are not, leave a message or don't" Beep...

Stillness.

Of Alabama, of home…

ALABAMA SUMMER

Cotton clouds swelled and spreading into a bright blue sky
Squinty eye sun so bright shining in my eyes,
Turn my head and close my eyes to still see the bright yellow orb of the
sun.

I look at the sky from left to right, little worms in my corneas dancing
Maybe scars from helter-skelter chases through briar patches
Or maybe a base-ball shiner

Sun on my forearms makes me remember,
A first chew of tobacco, and being as sick as a dog,
My first home run, the first time I stepped on a frog.

I remember the beginning of summer in the eighth grade,
The seniors all primping for a new life
Expecting a parade

Me with a ball glove, just waiting for the summer
To take long walks by Town Creek,
And go fishing with my little brother.

We built a raft in the woods and I caught poison oak,
I had my first drink of liquor,
Tried my first smoke

Boy Scout camp, a week away from home,
We greased watermelons and wrestled them in the lake
All kinds of new paths to roam

Yep, I remember that summer pretty well,
A baseball glove and the smell of fresh cut grass,
All my buddies with time to harass

Sunshine on my shoulders, but the time so quickly passes by,
Yet I still remember,
And sometimes can still cry:

For skin't knees and raspberry elbows,
For playing football in cow pastures,
When we were still young fellers

I still feel the sun,
And Lord have mercy
I still remember the fun..
Summertime…

COPPERHEAD CURVE

A packet of pictures sent through the mail
From my Momma to a mailbox
Passed through the fingers of her mailman,
Traveling clerk to clerk
Truck to truck, plane to plane
Alabama to New Jersey,
This packet of pictures traveling to me;

There is a mail slot in the front door of my house,
When I awoke, there on the floor the large yellow envelope
Momma's handwriting I recognized with a smile.
I carried the envelope in my hand as I went to start coffee
I laid it on the table in the dining room
While I stumbled still in sleep haze to the kitchen,
To fumble through cabinets in search of elixir fixins;

A cough and a sputter from the machine when the coffee began to brew,
I hear while searching for my favorite coffee cup.
The one with the University of Kentucky emblazoned on the front.
A gift from a friend missed and long gone;
Debating a breakfast and scratching sleep dust from my eyes,
I see the envelope from Momma sitting on the table; sweet anticipation.
Finally I pour a cup of coffee, light a cigarette, and pick up the paper vessel from home.

I love my Momma's hand writing, it is familiar from reading it all my life.
Even my name on the front of an envelope, in her script, makes me smile.
The coffee is hot and creamy; the cigarette even tastes good.
I look out the window of my dining room seeing spring's first finger-prints
Outside on the lawn I faintly hear the birds celebrating with song.

In the silence of morning do I hear the envelope ripping between my fingers;
Then greedily reach inside to pull out Momma's sendings.

The pictures are old. Black and white, and yellowed around the edges,
Pictures I have never seen, never knew existed.
Of Paw Paw when he was young and handsome, not a burden in the world.
Then one of Granny, she is smiling like a beam of light over the years,
To reach out to me in my kitchen, in a place she never visited.
Paw Paw again, older and still handsome, very dapper holding his Stetson.
I pour a fresh cup of coffee to help breech the decades between now and then.

I shift through to the last picture and catch my breath,
Set my coffee mug down with great care,
I light another cigarette because I have been transported so many years away.
There is the concrete porch of Granny and Paw Paw's cabin
I see the dark log support beam I had forgotten was ever there at all.
The metal rocker swing, I remember being a couch to spiders in the summer,
And the way the logs on the outside of the house were painted alternately green and white.

The screen door I recall slamming with glee until Granny hollered at me
Now I remember through this screen door was my heaven.
There was a coal stove in the living room before they switched to gas,
Out by the side of the house I remember is where coal was delivered and dumped,
A great pile of black chalky rock that was wonderful to a child,
You could climb to the top of it and roll off; you could break the soft rock on your head
Then you could walk into the house and get your butt beat for being

blacker than a spade.

Paw Paw had a bookshelf/cabinet in the living room, curved glass in small doors;
Inside he kept his wealth of Zane Grey novels and western magazines.
I think Paw Paw always fancied himself a cowboy and had a real Stetson
He was not afraid to wear anywhere, and usually did.
I remember holding his hat one time, and wondering if it would ever fit me.
Then I would grab the black and red felt hat he bought for me special
And ride my faithful broomstick pony all around the yard while he yelled "Don't let it buck ya son!"

Those were special times back then; I was so young I did not know I was young.
I remember one time setting a trap for a squirrel in the back yard;
I took a milk basket, propped one end of it up with a stick
Tied on about a hundred foot of string to the stick and threw a carrot under the basket.
And crawled over and hid by the house till a fat old squirrel got curious about that carrot.
He did, he capered down from a tree; then slowly found his way under the basket. I yanked that string!
I caught me a squirrel! And was awful proud of myself until I grabbed him; I still have a scar from that.

If you stood on the front porch and looked to the right you could see Uncle Obey and Aunt Dot's house.
Look to the left you saw the woods and where the dirt road curved. Copperhead Curve we called it.
Beyond the curve was where the Roger's lived, I used to go visit Tony.
Granny always told me when I was going to see him to watch out for copperheads.
Course, as soon as I got to Copperhead Curve, I always considered it my manly duty to hunt for them;

Which probably would have given her a fit if she were to know…
So I never told her.

I some how remember hot summer afternoons, strapping on plastic six-guns,
Putting my red and black felt hat on, the one Paw Paw got me special;
Then herding imaginary cattle and shooting outlaws all day long.
Every now and then I would climb a mimosa tree all sneaky;
And watch from the distance Aunt Dot walk through the garden to come visit Granny.
She knew Granny always had a big pot of coffee,
I would watch her until she got to the house, then think of some outlaw I needed to catch.

Sometimes those days seemed longer than a hundred years,
Then off in the distance I would hear a familiar rattle, and my heart would race,
Around copperhead curve would come Paw Paw's black Ford pickup truck.
I would find my broomstick pony and ride like the wind,
Cause here came Paw Paw, and he was my best friend.
I would ride my broomstick pony right up to his pickup just a whooping and a hollering cause he was home,
And when he shut the truck off I could hear crickets, because he always got home late.

I don't ever remember him not smiling. I don't ever remember not being happy with him.
He would get out of that truck and in a booming voice say "HOW YA DOING FLIPPER?"
He called me Flipper because of a television show I liked featuring a dolphin named Flipper.
Sometimes I would jump into his lap before he even got out of the truck.
There was never a kid happier his Paw Paw got home than me.

He'd push the red hat I was wearing off and tussle my hair,
He would ask if I had been a good cowboy and then ask if supper was ready, my Paw Paw.

Here I am again back in New Jersey. The coffee in my cup now cold;
I stand up feeling a little heavier, moving sort of slow.
I don't know how long I looked at that picture Momma sent me, the last one in the package.
I light another cigarette, pour another cup of coffee.
The picture was of another time; I had white blonde hair and was five years old or so,
Paw Paw had his arm around my little shoulder and I was leaning into him. Some picture.
I'm glad Momma sent it to me; I am already thinking of a frame.

Out here in New Jersey I don't worry about Copperhead Curve.
Now my broomstick pony has four wheels and I don't ride it for fun.
I am glad Momma sent me this envelope, I'm happy about the pictures;
But oh Lord I wish I could climb up one of Granny's Mimosa trees again,
And shoot them outlaws going after Aunt Dot as she walked through the garden.
Just one more time in time, the long time before this envelope came today,
Could I see Paw Paw's black Ford pickup truck coming around Copperhead Curve again.

POSTMAN

I received a letter
In the mail the other day
Slipped into my post-box from the hand of a man I did not know,
I guess it is the same man, or woman I suppose
Delivers my parcels every day
His or her name, I could not say.

This letter I held between my fingers,
The hand-script familiar,
The postmark old,
An envelope colored vermillion.

I opened it slowly, finger ripping along the outside edge,
I found myself in no hurry, time was my privilege.
Pulling the letter from the envelope, it made a sound like a paper whis-
per
And just for a moment, I experienced an otherworldly shiver.

I unfolded the pages, and gazed upon the script,
I read the sentences word for word, as tears began to drip
From my cheeks to the bonded page,
They came from my heart, my soul, and my age.

These words I had read before
In a different time, from a different shore
Funny how this life goes on
Never stopping or slowing a beat,
For as long as we are breathing, and on our feet;

I read each page from the start to the finish
Knowing each word, each written image
The words they spoke of love
They spoke of longing for some ones company,

They spoke of days cherished in memory.

I recognized each word, the handwriting I knew intimately
I looked up from my chair, through the dining room window,
From this vantage it is winter we are coming into
The colors of the lawn and trees;
Rather solemn I should say,
Quite befitting the mood I have achieved
After receiving this letter today.

I look back down upon the pages
Once again in recognition
For it is my handwriting I have been reading,
My sentences I am reliving.

I wrote this letter long ago when my father was still alive,
To ask him how he was doing, to tell him I was just fine;
Some how it never reached him
Never found its way into his hands
So he might read it, so he might understand
The times I did not visit or call to say hello
Did not mean I loved him less, I was just always on the go.

I wrote that indeed I loved him on the pages of this letter,
I explained how much I missed him and would try to do better,
I would make the time to see him; I would find the time to call
I would not allow the time to slip by,
Watching the colors change from summer to fall.

All within these pages I spilled my heart to him,
And now I find myself holding the same letter again
Except this time,
I have no address for the letter where I could send…

SHINY NICKELS

Momma told me, when she was a little girl
Her and Kay (Her big sister)
Would walk down the dirt road from their childhood home,
For a mile or more to go to Ross Robert's store

She said in the summertime when the dirt road was hot as a griddle,
When someone's truck or car passed you
However infrequent,
The dust would be so thick and swirling around her
She would have to look for Kay in its swath,
Thinking this might not have been a good idea.

Then the dust would settle
The rattle of the vehicle would fade into the distance,
She could feel the sun again
Cough out a little stream of brown spittle,
Knowing it "Weren't lady-like"
And then tag right along with Kay.

They walked down that road,
The security of innocence and rural life
Surrounding them with a protection difficult to imagine now,
There a neighbor on the porch waving a lazy hand,
Over by a pond a boy they knew fishing.

And they would walk this seemingly never ending dirt road,
On a trek,
To Ross Robert's store

They both had two nickels,
She told me Paw Paw would shine them, before he passed them to the
girls
Smile and say "Go on ahead to Ross's"

"Just git back before it's dark"

In the late afternoon on that quiet road,
Is where I often I imagine my Momma,
Wearing a little dress she would dust off occasionally
Just in case a neighbor looked real close,
Clutching shiny nickels her Daddy gave her,
And following Kay on a mini-adventure;

How sometimes those sharp pebbles on the road must have hurt her feet,
How pretty her little cheeks rosy in the sun must have been
In a time not thinking of me or my brother,
A little girl walking on a dirt road in Alabama with her sister,
Stopping now and then, to rest in the shade of a friendly oak tree

Then they would finally walk around that last curve in the road
Punctuated by another pond,
And on the crest of a hill
Stood Ross Robert's Store,
Red brick with picture windows, looking all cool inside.

I picture Momma and Kay
Bare feet marching into the store
Journey close to an end,
But with wide young girlish eyes staring at the rows of goodies,
Realizing it is about to begin.

Old Ross Roberts, with his almost gray hair and chubby smiling cheeks roared:
"Why, Kay and Jean! What brings you this way?"
"Does John Carlton know you done snuck out?"
He said it with a smile, and I know Momma with a shy smile said "Yes Sir"
While Kay just marched around looking like she owned the place, in

search of a candy bar.

Ross Robert's store was a cool place,
Even in the heat of the day, no way to really tell how,
Since back then was before air conditioning

Maybe it was the thickness of those red bricks made the building cool,
Or it sat over a spring, or maybe it was just country magic.
But whatever it may have been, Momma always remembered how cool
her feet were,
When standing in Ross Robert's store.

Momma and Kay would dig out their shiny nickels
And trade them in for a tiny candy bar and six ounce ice cold Coca-Cola
A tiny bell echoed in the store,
When Ross Roberts punched the tall buttons on the register
Then sprung out a drawer in which he placed the nickels in.

He held an almost white handkerchief and wiped the sweat off of his
forehead,
Very grandly saying: "Thank you ladies and come back again"
I imagine Momma giggling and maybe Kay grinning a little
As the girls chimed
"You're welcome" in perfect unison

Momma told me, when outside of that store,
She would eat that tiny candy bar,
Then drink the six ounce ice cold Coca-Cola,
And even to this day, over the multi-colored years to come and pass,
She remembered those as the best treats she'd ever had.

For two shiny nickels
One half a century ago,
That Paw Paw shined especially for her,
Her little teeth smiling,

Her little heart pounding, not knowing why until so many years past

Her little bare feet padding down the dirt road
Maybe her hand nestled in Kay's,
Late afternoon passing into evening;
Dragon flies stopping for a moment to look at her,
Then buzzing off to another interest,
My Momma swatting gnats from her little girl face…

The two little girls walking
Watching fire-flies in flight lighting like little Chinese lamps,
All over the place,
Starting to hear the crickets sing,
Hearing bullfrogs from the ponds answer in their mournful voices,
The two little girls walk all the way home.

UNCLE BUDDY

It was dark as hell that night,
There was woods all around but I couldn't see them
My friend and I was drunk on Raymond Ladd's homemade corn whiskey.
He said he made it in his bathtub,
And it tasted like an old dog wallered in it;
But it got you drunk…
Damn it was dark.

We walked over to the side of where the water went rushing over the
edge,
The edge of the Falls,
Desoto Falls.
We had drove around the chains so we could get over by the water;
Man it was dark,
And man were we drunk.

I eased myself over the rocks and then down to a ledge,
Looking all the way down to where the water disappeared into the noth-
ing below.
Country said: "Son, you're crazy, you gonna fall your ass over and we
ain't never going to find ya"
I heard, and sat on that ledge anyway.
Water roaring around me like a pissed off misty lion;
And I gazed over the edge.

Country climbed down and asked me what in the hell I was doing,
I said "Contemplating"
He said he only had a quarter, so I should save my fifty cent words,
I suggested he get naked with a goat.
We laughed, and he said "Really, what are we doing here?"
I said "You remember Uncle Larry?"

He said "Yeah, we went to the river with him a couple of times, right?"

I said:
"Yes. You see, Uncle Larry jumped off these falls,
And I'm sitting here contemplating doing the same"
Country said I was about a dumbass…but I wasn't.
I just wanted to be a little like my Uncle Larry.

I never jumped off those falls, and I will always wonder,
If I did, would I be as near as cool as my Uncle.
When I was a little kid running around the coal pile at Granny and Paw Paw's house,
Uncle Buddy would come tickle me and say there was at least one little nigger on Sand Mountain,
Then he'd go looking for some bacon and biscuits left over from breakfast;
Never seemed like he was around much, but when he was, he was like Elvis.
He always had a pretty girlfriend,
Used to say the prettiest ones are the craziest.
I didn't know what he meant back then,
I do now.
Lord I do now, although looking back,
I got lucky, I never married a Pat.

I remember him coming in late at night with a burlap sack full of frogs.
He'd smile at me and say "Someday I'll teach you to gig"
I'd just swell up and say I couldn't wait.
Then he'd go to the kitchen and watch frog legs jump out of the frying pan and laugh.
Uncle Larry, or Buddy, or Dillard,
I can't remember anyone in my childhood who smiled so much; and meant it.

He wasn't around much, but when he was,
He had a nice car and a pretty girl.
He was quick with a smile and quick to fight;

He never looked for trouble but taught a few lessons to those who did,
Uncle Buddy, on Sand Mountain.

He came to New York City to see me awhile ago,
We drank coffee and smoked cigarettes in Times Square and talked.
Let me tell you about my Uncle Buddy,
We were walking down 34th Street, and one of the kids suggested he climb the spire on the Empire State Building.
Uncle Buddy laughed and said maybe if he were ten years younger he would,
The difference between men is simply this: Uncle Buddy meant it…

So here I sit in New York City,
Drinking a beer, smoking a Marlboro thinking about a life a lifetime ago,
Thinking about my Mother's brother,
And oh brother, what a brother he is;
Some people talk about a favorite uncle,
But I got Superman, Elvis, and Hank Williams wrapped into one!

So all you city folk in your fancy shoes tromping down Broadway,
Keep in mind if Uncle Buddy's coming towards you,
Might want to step aside;
He might be a little grayer, he might not step as quick,
But let me tell you brother,
He might smile but he won't take a lot of shit.

This is my way of telling him,
You are something else my friend,
I know you don't hear from your city-fied nephew much,
But know he thinks of you often, and loves you much.
Uncle Larry, Uncle Buddy, Dillard,
I will never stand taller than your shortest shadow…

Love Regan

Of love, or something like it…

WINE GLASS

Sitting on the table, artistic in its solitude; a lone wine glass.
Barely seen to the naked eye, swirling on its smooth and cool surface,
Is your fingerprints; for last evening in your lovely hand did it rest,
And now this glass, alone and empty, is on my table without your grasp.

Last evening I watched this stemmed wine glass dance in the air be-
tween your fingers,
Just beyond its crystal rim was your whimsical grin, laughing at nothing
and smiling at me.
More intoxicating than the wine was your breathy kiss on my neck be-
low my ear,
The scent of grapes fresh upon your breath, as I looked into your eyes
and we shared a kiss;

Now my lonely wine glass is sitting on the table, surrounded by recent
memory;
Of you dancing in the candlelight, casting an alluring shadow upon the
wall
A simple glass turned complex in its presence, because you once held
it for a moment,
A moment too short, giving the promise of a memory lasting forever
long.

Empty wine glass when full seemed perfect in your hand, loving your
delicate touch
Delighting in your grip, even the wine chuckling in tiny waves as you
held it to your lips,
Sipping lightly a young chardonnay, sound of music soft in the room,
Outside the window the sound of a train passing as wine and lipstick
mingled; and I tingled.

Empty wine glass pristine in its solitude, graceful in its anonymity,
Alone on my table, its only company the morning sun passing through

its emptiness,
Remembering only the touch of your hand, fingers lightly caressing its
stem,
Empty and wishing only for the quick return of your touch again…

Stephanie.

CARTAS DE AMOR

I close my eyes tightly as eyelids will allow,
A darkness not dark, a light unseen
The beauty of nothing in this vacuum,
A darkness hoping for the light in nothing,
A Nothing hoping for something there,
There, which is, but is not, only fleeting.

I touched your skin turned velvet with hot water in the shower,
I tasted you.
Your kiss, your lips, your skin warm and smooth;
I tasted you into my thoughts.
I felt you in places,
In places,
Not usually touched; by you, your skin, or anyone at all…

And the water cascaded
Over your dark hair, blinked from your dark eyes,
Water washing over your breasts and thighs,
Washing from you and into my hair and my eyes;
My God
I breathe you in the water and see nothing but the blue and grey of life,
Your touch like damp silk, and moss growing in my inner forest

I attempt breathing in the water pouring off your body, choking on my breath,
Feeling your touch, your fingertips like paintbrushes stroking my skin,
Painting this moment, coloring my dreams, making me alive;
Making this moment,
This tiny moment in a torrent of hot water in a New York City shower,
Last forever…

We stand outside the shower
The water no longer running, the sound no longer deafening,

You, your long dark hair wrapped in a towel,
Me, standing wet and dripping;
Staring at you like some sculpture in Central Park,
Where we have danced before
The first time we kissed, the first time I tasted your lips,
And now from my shower you stand, beautiful.

You walk into the bedroom wearing my robe,
A towel wrapped over and through your hair.
I go to the kitchen and light a cigarette. Exhale smoke into the exhaust
fan on the stove,
I look at my fingertips holding it,
They are wrinkled and pruned from being in the shower with you,
I smoke the cigarette I know you hate,
With the knowledge five minutes from now,
The cigarette will not matter because,
I will be in your arms…

ISLAND GIRL

She was a Dominican girl,
Her smile like the reflection of an island sun;
And every time she smiled at me,
I felt as if life again had begun.

I'm older now,
It is not often I feel this way,
The girls they get younger,
As life and age makes you fade into gray.

But my God that smile!
Makes me remember my youth,
When holding her could have been in my grasp,
A desire now which belongs in the past,

My God she is beautiful!
A Dominican girl with a smile like the sun,
It is a smile I will carry forever,
Because she reminded what is like to feel young.

HOURS

Only hours until I see you again,
What is an hour?
Sixty minutes
Three thousand six hundred seconds
Yet,
Soon, but not soon enough

Hours,
A simple measurement of time
Of time passing
Waiting to gain;
A soft moment standing next to you,
For a second,
A minute
An hour.

Hours to wait,
Will fill some with sleep
Fill some awake,
Waiting for those moments
To spend time alone
With you
Without break

In a restaurant
In a café
In a minute waiting for a train.
Moments worth counting
Time spent like colors
A kaleidoscopic economy of minutes
Next to Jeanette

Hours

Time ticking by like errant rain drops
Falling, dripping from the crest of my umbrella,
Cannot count them all
Still
Watching the rain of time
Ticking and falling
By

Moments
Or hours,
Minutes lost in thought
Well worth the time spent weaving
Seconds spent daydreaming,
Of something as simple as,
Your smile.

Clock ticking tick tock,
Tomorrow soon but not soon enough
My contemplation soothing as music
In my thoughts, on my skin
In my dreams
Dreams of seconds passing too slowly,
To a tomorrow containing you.

Tick tock, tick tock
Clock ticking without stop,
Marching soldiers of seconds to attack a new day,
Sunshine and winter winds
Wrapping around you like a cloak
In my thoughts and you the queen,
Of tomorrows winter day.

Hours.
Dwindling down to minutes,

Trickling into seconds
Pooling to a puddle of moments

These are the things,
Separating you from me.

Hours

ASUNDER

Brown eyes, an almost crooked smile,
Used to have a boyfriend called them "Shark eyes",
Because nothing,
That's right. Just nothing
Was like those brown shark eyes.

Frosted blonde with big ideas,
She cries and laughs and wonders
Who could really love her?
When she truly comes asunder?

Under the covers she's by herself
Holding just a pillow
Thinking someone could fill her arms
Someone to be with her;

Another night winds slowly down,
A pillow in her arms;
Is not enough to fill her soul,
She cries far too long.

Frosted Blonde with big ideas
She cries and laughs and wonders:
"Who could really love her?"
When she truly comes usunder?

No Knight in shining armor,
Young Lochinvar cannot be found
In her bed she wonders,
If a Queen she could be crowned.

Slipping by the years they go
Passing like the day

She wishes for a meadow of gold
And someone she could share and hold.

Today has left and scarred again,
Those hopes she holds so dear
Surviving is the game she plays,
That's why she's still here.

Frosted blonde with big ideas
She cries and laughs and wonders
Who could ever love her?
When she truly comes asunder…

COLOUR

What's your favorite color Love?
What's your favorite song?
What kind of flowers on your mantle, do you long?

Where in your dreams do you sing?
Where in your heart are the things?
Your smiles and laughs and dreams.

Where my love? I want to know
Shall I plant the seeds where love might grow:

Gardens of flowers, colors row by row
Tiny bulbs that I may sew;
Tell me Love,
I need to know.

In sunsets grasp
Do you often gasp?
Of a passing suns twilight wonder.
Because a day not long has past
While you were still standing,
Wishing it to last;
Your life flashing far too fast.

So tell me Love, of your favorite colors
Whether lavender, pink or purples.
All the same or so it seems;
But what is special to you,
Shall be special to me;

I seek to find the flowers
For your mantle to adorn,
I want to be your favorite coat

The one threadbare and worn
That on chilly winter nights,
Keeps you comfortable and warm;

So, what's your favorite color Love?
What's your favorite song?
What kind of flowers Love?
Shall make the sacred bond?

So tell me Love, I need to know,
Of colors, flowers and things
Of that what makes you happy,
I will learn to sing.

MY SINGER

Slender fingers across an ivory keyboard tapping,
Red fingernails lifting and falling
Her eyes closed, she humming some song unknown
Her face a peaceful mask blissfully drawn
Searching and looking for an unknown song.

She hums and sings, just under her breath,
I watch her eyes shift under thin pink lids
Her lipstick patchy from the night, from the wine
And still she sings and sings
When she is not crying;

She throws her head back and lips slightly parted
Breaks into song…knowing the lyric is there,
But yet a tear rolls down her cheek, she stops to stare
There is not enough wine,
And the lyrics are too rare

Across the ivory keyboard she lays her slender fingers
A dribble of wine soaks her pretty chin
And then smashes the glass,
All crystal broken
She sobs for songs she knows unwritten.

Then she taps a certain key
Truth to be told,
Quite accidentally;
And she smiles,
A key of G.

"Hey…
I can work with that"
She closes her eyes and hums,
After letting her fingers over the keyboard be led,
She cleans up the wine and goes to bed.

TOMORROW

Tomorrow evening's when
I shall find the time
To love again:

When tomorrow morning comes,
Sun through the window shades
A warmth upon my brow,
But not here or now

Is exactly when,
I shall find the time,
To love again

In some spring afternoon
When multi-colored flowers,
Are in bloom

 And the shade is in my eyes from the willow tree
Touching my soul,
Making me free;

I know that then,
I shall find the time
To love again.

Summers sky blue and sweet
Browns my skin
A luscious heat,
Inside my head songs are singing
Inside my heart bells are ringing;

I know that is when,
I shall find the time

To love again

Falling leaves yellow and orange,
Scattered at my feet
Dropping gently from trees large

It is when,
I shall find the time,
To love again.

Winters touch, scratching cold
A promise of snows
Soon to unfold
Across prairies turned ivory,
The green a cold memory;

Maybe that will be when
I shall find the time
To love again.

ONE NIGHT

She:
New York City I am so tired,
Avery Fisher Hall before the Opera,
Maybe, just maybe, a drink,
I am tired, a cappacino,
Yes,
That would be good…

Me:
A nice day in the end of March,
The Ides of March aside,
This is not bad,
A night at the Opera..

How did we know?

A sky sunlit for a brief moment would swirl into black,
Of a night,
Walking together but apart,
Not knowing this night,
In its chill,
Would bring us together…..

The panorama opens, an African sky at Lincoln Center,
Casablanca lands lightly,
We had no idea,
You my Bergman,
Me your Bogie,
In the Rick's Café of our dreams.

With a scotch in hand I speak of Winter,
Snowflake,
A memory revisited,

Not knowing the chill touched you at my side,
Your glance over the steam of your cup,
I wanted to talk to you,

And we spoke.
Betty delicate and beautiful next to me,
A hint of dreams not quite forgotten in her perfume,
Elegant as polished silver and diamonds,
Voice like crystal massaged,
Betty.

I did not know her, but was compelled,
To find out who she was,
And time danced to the script on the tickets we held,
An Opera to see,
We had to part.

We walked across the courtyard,
Where not long ago was the fountain,
Speaking to each other and to the wind,
Not holding hands but wanting to,
The elegance of her as consuming as the night.

I smoked a cigarette,
She said she loved the smell,
I looked at her quizzically,
She said, "Some things in life you never forget,
Years, events, in 1978 in Milan I stopped smoking,
It caused wrinkles,
But to this day I still love the smell",
I smiled,
We went to the Opera.

She to her seat,
Me to mine,

Three acts,
Puccini,
Tosca,

I thought of her at intermission,
I sipped my scotch smoking a cigarette,
On the balcony at the New York Opera,
Looking at Broadway, watching Taxi cabs drift by,
And then went on to finish the Opera.

Tosca.   Where we met…

As I was leaving,
Weaving my way through the crowd to 66th street,
My phone rang,
It was Betty,
She said I want to give you long kisses,
I said,
Is there any other kind?

And now we talk…

SILLY BUTTERFLY

Silly butterfly stretches her wings in flight,
Sun shining through wings, her colorful dress,
Silly butterfly floating on the breeze,
Her dreams and the dreams of the sky flowing together

Silly butterfly lights softly on the top of a bottle of Chardonnay
Trembles her wings and sniffs the air,
Flies off in a golden pirouette,
Looking for the cork of a Pinot Noir, she wants a red.

Look into the sky, look into the air
Barely see her gliding about your hair
A little halo only for you, multicolored and true,
Silly butterfly flying, silly butterfly flying,

Flying, gliding and floating just beyond your vision,
She banks and tumbles,
The colors of her wings flashing,
Like so many Crayons spilling from a box.

Silly butterfly, a painting in the wind,
The sky the tapestry she paints her colors
A dab of gold, a dab of blue, a dab of red and orange,
Silly butterfly cart-wheeling on a sigh, coloring the sky,

What is she thinking? The trees ask among themselves
"She is not," replies the brook bubbling around moss covered stones
And the grass speaking like the shifting winds, said:
"She is not thinking, she is what a child's laughter would look like."

So she lights upon a leaf, then dances with a flower,
She whirls and she twirls, flying with abandon,
Worshipping a sun which lights her wings like happy fire,

Silly butterfly flies colorfully towards night not tiring.

She met with lady-bug and they had a discussion,
On who's orange was oranger, who's back had a better design,
Then they frolicked in the air as if time had paused only for them,
The squirrels held their breaths in wonder, a wily old beaver smiled.

Silly butterfly flying, in love with the wind
Never a tear to mar her passing, just a flick and a flutter,
The tiniest rush and bustle of wings flapping,
A Queen in her sky castle, the tiny Lady of the Manor;

Silly butterfly flying: flying into sky,
Into the hearts of all who pause to watch even briefly,
Silly butterfly flying, flying into the sky,
Into my heart and then on into the night

Iron your dress Silly Butterfly...

NOVEMBER DANCE

In the gloom and chill of the winter moon
You in my arms we shall dance the dance of the November winds,
Beneath the shadows of the boughs of leafless trees
Waltzing in a snowy realm
Spinning on beds of crunching leaves;

The bareness of the fall
Mixed with the heat and passion of human desire
In the night we build in a mist
To warm us an icy fire,
We shall always burn in winter, burning merrily together
Laughing to mortality, the heat of our spirits un-tethered

Glint of moonlight flashing off your smile,
Upon my neck your breath hot and moist
The cold all but forgotten
In our winters dance, in a devilish trance
Chasing and gaining but never quite attaining,
A November romance...

Life and its happenings…

AM 1 TRAIN

Tired faces, tired shoes
Looking at as if reading Vanity Fair
On the 1 train
Tired face she is
Leaning on her husband,
Tired husband pretending not to lean on her

The whoosh sounds of a late night train,
Everyone leaning to and fro with the train motion,
He pretends to read Vanity Fair,
Acting interested, flipping through pages,
Holding his wife, hoping for home soon

Tired faces, tired shoes,
Pretending to read Vanity Fair,
On the 1 train
At one thirty in the morning,
Tired faces, tired shoes.

What do they see?
A five dollar magazine in his hands,
No hope in his face,
Turning the pages,
Pulling a glossy tri-fold advertisement delicately,

Tired faces, tired shoes,
Some wearing smiles like masks,
Some in wary slumber, some already a memory to themselves,
Tired faces, tired shoes,
On the 1 train….

BIG GIRL

She sat on a stool looking across the bar into a mirror seeing nothing
When asked, she ordered a Jameson on the rocks.
Her makeup while not modern, was precisely applied
I gave her the Jameson and took her money
She was demure and sad, soft spoken in a tired sort of way.

Her fingernails were crudely polished silver
Reminding me of childhood attempts at painting model airplanes
I asked if she were okay,
A whisper between lipsticked lips she said it had been a bad day,
I suggested another Jameson might help; she said Jameson was the standard.

She was overweight yet still dressed attractively
Hiding curves in folds of clothing, a peek of a silk bra,
A furtive smile, badly gapped teeth
Her small lips painted in such a way you knew she had concentrated on them,
She produced a five dollar bill in asking for more Jameson.

I wondered as all bartenders wonder I suppose,
What story this girl was hiding behind her eyes
While providing her with, and watching her drink,
Her very grown-up drink of Jameson on the rocks
I watched her sigh around a red cocktail straw.

She spoke little to me, though I watched as she spoke to the hounds,
The same ones who are in from night to night,
I feared for her,
Considering the hounds semi-drunken appetites
She ordered her own Jameson's, she would be alright.

Long dark hair dropping in dripping curly cues about her shoulders

Not unattractive in the damp pulsating neon bar lights,
Her makeup not modern, but precisely applied
A little overweight girl, slipping through another lonely night,
In my bar…drinking Jameson on the rocks.

O'Connell's
Where the broken come to gather
When you begin to feel the night start dragging at your eyes
Come join us in commiseration;
We'll commiserate together.

A scotch and a beer
With all their tales of woe,
Do they gather
We'll gather together to share broken tales
Or not talk at all.

Drinking with themselves, with ourselves
Talking, not talking, drinking our souls
Thinking,
Something more than here,
Something brings the misery.

O'Connell's
Pub to the world of broken men,
You've seen a pub like this
Maybe even you've been in one,
Where the laugher is not merry,

Where the broken gather together;
O'Connell's Pub
Somewhere around 108th and Broadway
Where the only songs come from the juke box…

But the beer is,
Cold
And there is ice for your whiskey
In the gather of the broken;
A cold drink is more welcome than the sun…

BUG

Little bug,
Who alights on my book:
Don't be shy little friend
Have a look.

I was alone,
Till you dropped by
Just reading poetry,
Just killing time;

But now you are here,
Little wings preening
I welcome your company
Amidst my dreaming.

Such a small and delicate thing,
Are you little bug
A wisp of life,
A tiny drop of blood,

God is truly genius
In creating you,
Little bug,
And away he flew…

CASING

The casing of logic,
Nothing but the bone of a skull
Rocks and trees and dogs
Do not seek truth.
That skull is but a casing,
Of so many ponderous thoughts
Is human just human?
In folds of brain is where logics caught.

I wonder why I am
More than blood and tissues and life,
I protest I have a soul
I seek a God,
A creator, a father a reason,
For this casing
Proposing logic
Questioning life;
I am Man.

I am so presumptuous to consider,
I have more reason or purpose or goals
Than a mindless spider seeking a moth
A spider without a soul
A purpose or goal,
Says I:
Man
In my casing of logic

I will step on a beetle and swat a fly
For these soulless creatures
Are pestering I,

No casing of logic

Do they possess;
They may have a casing
But no logic,
I guess.

They hinder my mood
And comfort
And die
For their trouble;
I am Man.
It is fine
I'll steal their life:
For their lack of logic
Is my vindication.

No logic in the rocks
No logic in the streams,
So I will alter their course
In fulfilling my dreams…
Says I:
Man.
Possessor of logic
In a casing,
Just above my shoulders.

Killing and death
The footprints I'll leave;
And murder is not murder,
If done properly;
Logically,
Says I,
Man.
I will always sleep well
Having a casing of logic,
Where I might dwell,

My casing of logic
Allows me to create,
Comfort, luxury…
And hate.

I am Man,
And that is answer enough
In my casing of logic;
I will justify,
Any injustice,
Any aberration
Says I!
I am Man
Is my cry!
But if not for a casing of logic,
Would I weep?

But in weeping is no wonder,
And wonder is what I need
I think in death I will be the thunder
Arrogance is my name,
Says I:
Man.

So in this casing of logic,
Oft times I simply tremble.

CENTRAL PARK

If time was the sky,
I am waiting for the clouds to break and you to appear…

I walk in step with the clip-clop of horse's hooves on pavement,
The rhythm of the carriage,
Central Park on a Sunday in the fall;
The happy music of a carousel,
A wet translucent bubble floating on air explodes on my knuckles,
Children running,
Children laughing
Wooden steeds merrily painted and awaiting their journey,
Tiny hands holding tightly to silvery poles,
The anticipation staining faces not yet creased by life.

Play music play!
Oh music play.

A musical world spinning slowly round and round,
Giant dreams escaping tiny heads,
Sitting atop armored steeds,
Rushing into fantasy battles,
Up and down, round and round,
Turn carousel turn.

Play music play!
Oh music play.

Chariots pulled by painted ponys,
Start to move around
And around,
Up and down,
Tiny hands holding on;
Smiles like sunshine,

Faster and faster they turn!
Louder and louder they laugh!
Spinning carousel.

Play music play!
Oh music play.

Sunday afternoon in Central Park,
In the fall;

Play music play!
Oh music play.

And the universal language of children screaming with joy,
Fills the air,
More music.

Now ice-skaters surrounded by trees and city,
Some gliding with ease,
Some sliding on their knees;
One skating with grim determination,
All on white ice beneath a blue sky
A young couple on awkward feet, skating anyway,
Holding hands,
Smiling at one another.
The squeesh and scrape, the sounds of blades,
Scraping over ice,
Feet precariously sliding on wobbly ankles,
A man waving his hands before falling on the ice,
Sliding on his back,
The Beatles playing from hidden speakers;
Voices, voices rising from the ice,
Languages different but the same.
Another man falls,
And does a balancing dance trying to get up,

Laughing heartily as he stands,
To wipe ice from his blue jeans.
Pink Floyd is now singing into the air,
Skaters everywhere,
Skating.

My my,
Central Park on a Sunday afternoon,
In the Fall.

And again I walk...

There is a little girl running, pink stockings flashing,
To an even smaller brother,
She screaming through a smile "Bubby!"
The hair on his little head wisps of blonde,
A mans haircut on a little boy,
Sister loves her Bubby,
Precious
A little dog is yapping and prancing around their little feet,
A happy ball of fur full of energy,
Mother yelling "Come here Sassi!"
Little dog paying no mind,
Father in his blue jean jacket,
Camera in hand,
Guarding his brood.

Again I walk...

A lady stands alone
On the stone foot-bridge;
Gazing into the green water and the looming city,
Smiling at nothing and everything,
The wrinkles on her face proclaiming,
I have lived!

She walks away.
Another woman poses for a picture,
I hear her say "My bangs are a mess"
The woman posing with her says:
"You look great"
They smile,
A camera flashes,
Now they are there forever.

Central Park on a Sunday afternoon,
In the Fall.

And I walk…

The pool of water beneath the bridge so closely reflects the sky,
You would not jump in without a parachute,
A lady strolls by telling her husband she is hungry,
Heels clacking,
A grandmother sits on a wooden bench holding an infant,
Patting the tiny blanketed back,
A dot upon her forehead suggesting she is Indian,
Tiny baby wrapped in a blanket whiter than snow.
Voices float by,
I think they are Russian,
But who knows?

I walk,

Lovers are walking,
Some holding hands,
Some arm in arm,
 A young man casually drapes his arm across the shoulders of his girl;
So many ways of touching,
All holding onto,
Not wanting to lose that feeling,

Of love.
A procession of carriages,
Drivers wearing top-hats holding faux whips,
All with black horses,
Clip-clopping by…

Central Park on a Sunday afternoon,
In the Fall.

A thousand birds or so it seems,
Fly overhead like little circus performers,
Swirling in ranks,
To settle noisily into a tree,
Causing the leaves to ripple like waves on a lake,
And then, still.
I sit on a bench to write,
A little dog with long white hair stops by to say hello,
Sniffs my shoe and winks his eye,
And then keeps walking down the path,
Just like me.

Time to go, the afternoon is waning,
I walk from the path towards the street,
Now I begin to hear traffic,
Horns and squeals and squeaks and sirens;
The bird's songs are fading,
I walk up the stairs at the end of this path,
And like magic,
There is Fifth Avenue.
The end of an afternoon, the end of my walk,
What a lovely Fall day to take a stroll,
In Central Park on a Sunday;
My eyes feel funny, only a tingle,
Not really tears I tell myself,
I hail a yellow cab,

We pull into the traffic,
A canoe winding through canyons of buildings,
In the spongy black back seat I whistle to myself an old tune,
Amazing Grace…

TORTURED SOUL

I have a tortured soul
Might not have always been.
Don't remember what I was born with,
The Baptist's say was sin,
A little tiny baby crying for Mommas tit,
Seems an odd sort of sin to me.
The Baptist's also speak of mysterious ways,
In which the Lord works,
But I still don't think tiny babies are sinful.

I have a tortured soul,
I wonder of many things,
Always too stubborn to take someone else's word for things,
Would rather find out on my own.
Finding out later, sometimes,
Should have just taken that word;
Could have saved time, money, and maybe,
A piece of soul;
But who knows?

I have a tortured soul,
Not complaining mind you,
Just pointing out:
Sometimes my early mornings
Seem blacker than the night before,
And sometimes in the night before,
I prayed fervently to my maker,
To just take me in the dark,
Somewhere forever is good.

I have a tortured soul,
Don't know why,
Same as it's always been,

The drip of a tear in laughter,
A grimace behind my smile;
Oh, it's not all bad,
I have lived a life of the happy gypsy,
Forever climbing hills to see the other side.

It's just,
I have a tortured soul,
Who knows why?

JOURNEY OF THE DAMNED

Across the river Styx I row, arms like molten lead
Going to the place of the damned, where all the fallen tread
A place of pain so soon to reach, place of morbid dread
Across the river Styx I row; to the place undead.

I thought while breathing easily, in a life passed by so quickly
The myth of hell and damned forever was a fable for the sickly,
The Zealots spoke of happy places, filled with gold and smiling faces
I laughed and scorned their simple faith; and now row to my fiery fate.

What Pearly Gates? With mirth I questioned. Some astral place I could not envision,
Wondering of what to become while scorning where I might have gone,
To laugh in the heavens I might have known, but lust for life created scorn
My time was short and now I know; arms tired from rowing and worn.

The River Styx a long, long road; but short so short compared to Eternities load,
So row and row and row I do, in deaths never ending tide
To a far off shore I too soon will reach
Be cast upon a flaming beach.

No God nor caring Son shall then remember
Anything I was will not linger,
Listen to my painful cry…arms leaden rowing to another side,
Your life is once and never risk…losing it to the River Styx.

MIRRORS

My suggestion is only a suggestion
Place another mirror
Ten paces
Directly across from the mirror on your wall
Step to the side of either mirror
And gaze into one to the other.

Look down the endless corridor of mirrors
Until into the mirror distance of mirror reality
A speck of a person you think you see
The shadow of someone
You can barely detect:

This someone far, far away
Standing in the mirror corridor you are looking into
This someone you spy
That someone is me;
Hiding in your mirrors
For only you to see

Remember,
My suggestion,
Is only a suggestion
For the mirror corridor
Has captured;
More than one butterfly...

It's new songs man;
There's always new songs,
And people singing;
Like no one has ever sang before.
All the new songs
There is always more,
And the music touches inside
Where you cannot hide
Even from yourself,
New songs
The time it goes slowly by
It should drag but man it flies!
And all the seconds tick off the clock
You are getting older but you are not;
Because of new songs
They keep you young.
The time turns into tears
Washing away your fears
Of life;
New songs
The lyrics flow and mold,
They are the same but not.
New songs
Ticking and ticking the time
Going far, far away,
But never having left,
New songs;
Singing like never before
And then it is someone else's turn,
To sing and play and feel,
The new songs;
You let go before you know
There was never anything to grip at all.

And in a blink you stop and you think
You know there can't be wrongs
Drifting through this gig called life,
Because there are new songs,
New Songs.

ON ROBERT BURNS STATUE IN CENTRAL PARK

Robert Burns sits pondering,
On a pedestal in Central Park,
Quill in hand he seems pensive and wondering,
Why in all places,
Did he land here in Manhattan.

The Fall is the nicest,
I would want to hear him think,
Its golden, green, and skylight blue,
But he sees every season.

When the chill is so sharp no person known,
Strolls past this reverential prison,
And birds are just memories of echoes bouncing off stones,
The cold of winter Mr. Burns endures.

A warm breath of wind in February,
Causes the sounds of ground crunched by heels,
And Robert yet again,
Has reason for his quill,

There is time between March and July,
With wind and rain, with cold and snow,
Robert sits as a firm stoic,
Waiting for the human voices,
He found melodic.

I take his picture, a handsome statue,
Wondering while the wind flows around me,
I find him precious now,
Did I find him or he find me?

SEPTEMBER DAY

Manhattan sky the end of a September day,
Upper West side,
106th and Broadway.

Clouds like fluffy white stains on a black sky,
Upper, Upper West Side.

Black man with a cane,
Rattling a Starbucks cup,
Please, please, I need to eat,
Ambushing people coming out of Duane Reade.

An English bulldog trying to make friends with a poodle,
The owners exchange pleasantries,
Will she bite?
Oh no, she loves everyone!

Bulldog wriggling with happiness,
Poodle a dirty marshmallow wagging her tail,
Grey haired lady on one leash, yuppie on another.

Upper Upper West side,
End of September,
In New York City..

THE 1 TRAIN

I sat on my orange plastic seat on the One train,
Scotch running through my head, a hazy vision looking out
Reading my book,
Needing to clean my glasses
Didn't matter, vision a little foggy anyway

I looked up over the frame of my spectacles
Spying on my train mates,
And across from me sat a boy and a girl,
He so young the pimples still angry on his face,
She looking at him with a look I can only describe as love.

He was reading from an open school book
Finger tracing the points he was making,
Her watching and listening with awe
These kids on the One train
Hurtling towards the Bronx

She looked at him and kissed his cheek,
He leaned into her almost imperceptibility.
She is beautiful and he knows,
She kisses him,
And he glows.

She is listening to her ipod, nodding her head to the beat,
She takes one plug from her ear and places it into one of his,
He smiles and for a moment looks at her,
Then turns his face away, tucks the book into the backpack at his feet,
They smile at each other.

The train begins to slow
From 125th street entering into 137th City College,
She looks longingly into his eyes and kisses his cheek,

I see the haunting cast in his eyes as he leaves her on the train,
As I walk next to him as this is my stop.

Oh Jeanette,
I watched the love of youth played out on the One train,
I saw the look in those children's eyes,
I understood the feeling they shared,
And I thought of you.

TUESDAY

Frequently the mornings shuffle, like cards overlapping end to end
The sun hides behind and colors clouds purple and gold,
Waiting for the afternoon to descend
Birds they sing and soar into the day
Squirrels dance and frolic in tree's defying the wind.

A crow passing by caws a raspy hello
Seemingly chuckling at those on the ground below,
And the tentative green buddings on trees hoping for spring,
Will in the early morning make sparrows sing.

A cat creeping slowly through the neighbor's hedge,
To itself so invisible, crafty and cunning
Until a sharp noise from traffic sends the yellow tabby running,

The sun through the branches and over the roof next door,
Makes me whimsically happy needing no more;

In my dreams so rarely possible is this spectacle to see
Me staring at a waking and walking family not noticing me
And there they going, believing unseen
But not this sunny morning, they are watched and seen by me.

A Tuesday is so rare to be remembered, or any day or time,
Yet today is a Tuesday to rest in memory sublime
No bird upon my shoulder, no grass massaging the soles of my feet
Just me and my window…and a Tuesday so sweet.

WEDNESDAY

I had a sambuca for breakfast in the middle of the afternoon,
In a bar named P.D. O'Hurleys off of west 72nd street,
The chilly fingers of a witch named winter scraping my face,
With promises to come, as October draws towards the darkness,
Impending rain in the air.

I toss a cigarette into the street as a cab speeds by,
A black man in a blue windbreaker asks me for change,
A young girl in knee-high leather boots walks by,
Pouty lips,
My oh my, New York City's Upper West Side.

Bar is full of firemen,
Been there awhile,
Irish accents raised in mirth,
Ties undone, or off dress uniforms
Sharing camaraderie and whiskey as only men who walk with death
daily can.

Babies in strollers being pushed by the open window,
Guided by their parents distraction;

Young people, old people, crippled people
All walk by, or roll, or limp or crawl;
Some in a rush
Some in a wander,
Some barely there.

I hear the noise of a bus,
Sip my drink,
Turn my head and watch it roll by

Like a great painted whale in this ocean of a city,

Stopping briefly:
People get on,
People get off,
People hold tightly to their seats

Just like life.

And in the bar,
People walk in,
People walk out...

People sitting on their barstools like royalty upon the throne
Laughter and conversation swirling in the air
Music from an unseen juke box...

Hands raising glasses,
Eyes watering from whiskey dew
A pretty bar-maid with dyed hair askew,
This is a contented loneliness;
My oh my,
Wednesday afternoon,
On the Upper West Side...

And again, we are at the end of something. Many years ago I was on a Subway train, I don't remember the line. Directly across from me there was a drama playing out between an Asian couple who looked to be in their fifties. I did not understand the language they were speaking, but I fully understood the emotions. She was angry, and he was distraught. The train stopped at Canal Street and the lady rushed off with the man shortly following. For whatever reason, the train sat briefly before the electronic bell dinged announcing the doors would close. I watched the woman rush up the stairs leading to the street. The man was in tears yelling after her, his foreign words echoing through the station, he stopped at the beginning of the stairs watching her disappear upon the steps above him, and with one hand on the safety rail of the staircase, he lay his head upon his arm and began to sob. This is when the train doors closed, and we began moving through the tunnel. I turned my head and watched his misery for one more brief moment and then we were gone into the flashing lights and darkness of the tunnels. In my mind I shuffled the possibilities. He had been caught cheating on her? but they seemed to be an age past such infidelities. Perhaps it was a business deal gone awry, but the emotion seemed too high for that. I had watched her, and could tell she was the one betrayed, and he, the betrayer. Was he an alcoholic who abused her? She didn't seem abused. He was in the wrong and it was written all over his face and actions, she was not so much fed up, as putting a period on a sentence only they knew what was. Did he gamble away their savings? Was he a drug addict? Did I read the whole scenario incorrectly? Was she leaving him after a long marriage where she was the adulterer and he wanted nothing more than to hold on to the only anchor he had ever known? Who knows? But it is the job, no, the responsibility of the writer, to consider these things; and the poet to obsess over them.

I will never know what really happened between that couple; but I will always remember them for the emotion they reflected, it was like the sun off of polished glass. And that is writing. It is not the words, it is the thoughts, and these words are an attempt, a poor and slighted attempt, to explain and highlight the emotions of the human heart; but with words we do it on paper, the real thing tingles upon the skin. And my hope is simple: I hope there are words I put on paper, which make you tingle upon the skin. Thanks for sticking around folks, and like I end every evening I will say this, "G'nite Amanda, the grey wolf is headed towards the pod."

Martin Regan Dove
October 19, 2013
New York City

CPSIA information can be obtained at www.ICGtesting.com
Printed in the USA
LVOW10s1745120715

445937LV00002B/3/P